"Doris Davis tells a very believable story about a fascinating time in Egyptian history. Although the story is fictional, it ties together many of points of fact and speculation relating to the times of Akhenaton and Tutankhamun. Ms. Davis creates a picture of life in ancient Egypt that few other sources provide. I highly recommend this book."

Dr. Robert B. Pickering
DENVER MUSEUM OF NATURAL HISTORY

MARCO POLO LIBRARY

Flower of the Nile

by
Doris Auger Davis

*Marco Polo Passengers:
With compliments of
the author.
Doris Auger Davis
March 31, 2000*

Copyright © 1998   Doris Auger Davis

All rights reserved.
Reproduction of any part of this book,
without the expressed consent of the author,
is strictly prohibited.

First Printing, 1998

Printed in the United States of America

Illustrated by Doris Auger Davis

Scott Grimes
was commissioned for cover design
and illustration refinement

D.A. Davis, Publisher
P.O. Box 441252
Aurora, CO 80044-1252

For my daughter, Jenny,

Grandchildren, Meralee, Monica and Jim

and

My dear husband, Henry.

For proof-reading the manuscript
and making suggestions to
enhance the accuracy,
grateful appreciation and many thanks
are extended by the author to:

Robert B. Pickering, Ph.D.,
Department Chairman
Anthropology Department,
Collections and Research Division
DENVER MUSEUM OF NATURAL HISTORY
Denver, Colorado

ANCIENT EGYPT

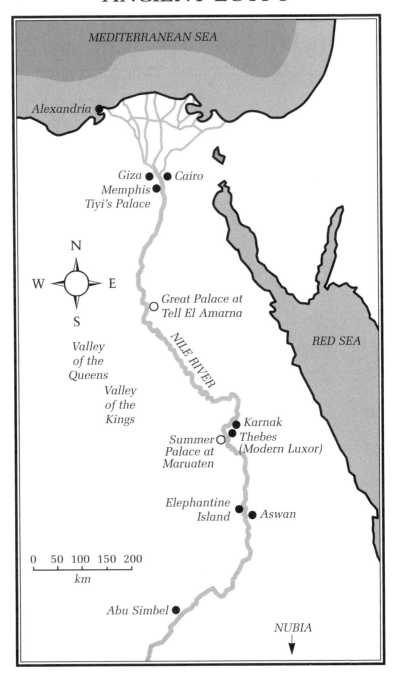

FORWARD

I have spent much of my adult life traveling the world. Of all the countries I have visited, one stands out and captures my fascination and imagination above the others. That country is Egypt. I have experienced the heat and sweat of Giza. I have climbed the torturous ladder leading to the burial chamber of the Great Pyramid. I have stood before the empty granite sarcophagus that once contained the remains of the Pharaoh Khufu about four thousand seven hundred years ago.

Wandering through tombs and temples that have withstood the ravages of time, puts one in a very humble frame of mind.

Traveling by riverboat to such places as Luxor, the Valleys of the Kings and Queens, Nag Hammadi, Dendera, Esna, Kom Ombo, Aswan and Elephantine Island, and flying to Abu Simbel, helps to erase the memories of the intestinal "curse" commonly associated with cruising the Nile.

Visiting the Antiquities Museum in Cairo and viewing the treasures of Tutankhamun, one is led to question how all those objects could have come from such a small tomb. Only by studying the pictures and drawings of Howard Carter and his team can a true understanding emerge.

At the time I entered the tomb of Tutankhamun, I had no doubt it was the genuine place. A strange feeling of awe swept over me as I stood in the empty Antechamber. When I climbed the wooden steps that had been added later for tourists to view the Burial Chamber, I was entranced with the painted walls and the sarcophagus in the middle of the room that held the remains of Tutankhamun in one of his original wooden coffins.

Later, while I studied this period in Egyptian history, images of the family of Tutankhamun formed in my mind. The imagination can indeed play odd tricks on an otherwise practical mind.

The story, I seemed compelled to write, takes place almost three thousand three hundred and fifty years ago. Some of the names and places are real, and some are not. Tutankhamun did marry Ankhesenamun. Nefertiti was the wife of Akhenaton. Smenkhkare, Meritaten, Ay, Tiyi, Horemheb and Schubbuliliuma did exist at that time. Tahlia, Abdul, Anwar, Farida and Tashery are fictional. There was a place called Tell El Amarna, and Thebes was the ancient capital at one time. The chapters dealing with the pyramids and the Sphinx, Karnak, religion, the mummy, the tomb treasures and the burial are true as described in the list of reference books. I drew my own sketches.

Some of the dates are open to scholarly debate, but all are within the approximate time frame dictated by history.

The tomb had been broken into at least two times, possibly three. Gold was the most desired loot, but oil also was precious to the ancient Egyptians. Vessels of oil had been emptied. They were removed from the tomb by filling leather containers. These were passed to fellow robbers in a dirt tunnel that had been dug above the long passageway leading to the Antechamber. All four rooms of the tomb had been plundered; but, fortunately, the Great Wooden Shrine in the Burial Chamber remained intact.

An interesting fact was that the chests of clothing and other items in the Antechamber had been hurriedly rearranged. On top of some of the chests, hieroglyphs spelled out their contents, but someone, pressed for time, returned them to the wrong chests without reference to the hieroglyphs. *An unknown person had tried to put this room in some kind of order.* Who could have done this? Perhaps a grandfather out of love for his grandson? One who could control further break-ins of the tomb — one with the power of a Pharaoh?

As to the "curse" of the tomb, this was possibly started by the media to make the discovery more intriguing. There was no statement about a curse of any kind on the walls of the tomb; in fact, the Burial Chamber was the only room with paintings and revelation of the religious ceremony for the burial of the king. Also, no scrolls of any kind were found in the tomb.

These examples of Amarna period art will always be a gift to us by exposing us to these wonderful treasures. The creativity of the ancient Egyptian artisans continue to fascinate us even to this day.

At least three autopsies have been performed on the remains of Tutankhamun over the seventy-five years since his tomb was discovered. At this time (1998), his mummy has been returned to the Valley of the Kings. Let us hope that he can now rest in peace.

This is a fictional novel. The human element is my own. I sincerely hope the reader will find it enjoyable and helpful in understanding that exceptional ancient culture.

I also hope that the reader will some day have the same fortunate opportunity as I to visit that wonderful land of enchantment... Egypt.

The Author

CHARACTERS

ANKHESENAMUN - "Anie"

TUTANKHAMUN - "Tut"

NEFERTITI - The Queen

AKHENATON - The King

TAHLIA - Ankhesenamun's Nubian Servant

AY - High Priest and Grandfather

TIYI - The Queen Mother

ANWAR - Tutor and Scribe

MERITATEN - "Meri"

SMENKHKARE - "Smenke"

TASHERY - The Child

ABDUL - Tahlia's Friend

FARIDA - Tashery's Attendant

SCHUBBULILIUMA - The Hittite Prince

CONTENTS

Chapter		Page
1	During the Reign of Pharaoh Akhenaton	1
2	Journey to the Banks of the Nile	7
3	Egyptian Religion	23
4	Anwar	35
5	Pyramids and the Sphinx	43
6	War and Incest	61
7	Tashery	69
8	Karnak	83
9	The Royal Wedding	99
10	The Reign	109
11	Tragedy Strikes	127
12	The Plan	135
13	The Mummy	143
14	Final Preparations	155
15	Valley of the Kings and the Wreath of Flowers	163
16	Entombment, Intrigue and Flight	181
Appendix		195

SKETCHES

PALACE AT TELL EL AMARNA xii
TUTANKHAMUN'S TOMB
IN THE VALLEY OF THE KINGS 164
TUTANKHAMUN'S TOMB 168
YELLOW QUARTZITE SARCOPHAGUS 176
THE FOUR SHRINES 184
THE OUTERMOST GREAT WOODEN SHRINE .186
COMPLETION OF BURIAL 188

Egypt

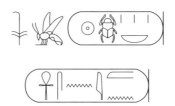

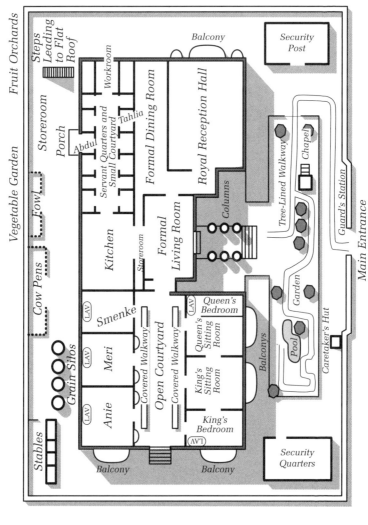

1

1337 B.C.

DURING THE REIGN OF PHARAOH AKHENATON

Crouching behind a bush and believing that she cannot be seen, Anie suddenly feels a slap on her back. A shout of, "You're it!" floods her with surprise and delight. She gets up quickly. It's her turn to face the tree with her hands over her eyes and to count to ten slowly. Peeking ever so carefully through her fingers she can see her brother and sister running as fast as they can to a selected hiding place. Then, all is silent.

This beautiful garden is part of one of the courtyards that is within the grounds of the great Egyptian palace situated at Tell El Amarna. This is where the Pharaoh Akhenaton and his family reside in the year 1337 B.C. To protect these members of the royal family, a high wall made of sun-dried mud bricks and painted white encompasses the entire complex. Security for their safety is of utmost importance.

The courtyard, situated near the entrance, snuggles protectively inside lower walls. An opening from it leads towards the entrance of the palace itself which stands majestically in the center. Swaying palm trees line walk-ways on either side.

Bright sun is spreading itself evenly over the vast countryside. It flows like a warm blanket into the garden. It is a beautiful place. The rows of thick green foliage are interrupted ever so often with patches of flowers that have been carefully planted in bright multi-colored hues. They catch the sun's rays and sway in the warm breezes, their heads bobbing as if in communication with one another. An unevenly-shaped placid pool reflects the blue sky, obstructed only by the white lilies dotting its surface.

"Now! Ready or not!" Just as she leans over and starts to push back a clump of bushes, a voice calls from a nearby balcony. "Anie! Come at once!"

There is a moment of hesitation. "And bring Meri and Smenke with you."

It is the queen, their mother, calling and waving to them. The bright glow of the day leans against her face to reveal rare beauty. Her name, Nefertiti, means "The Beautiful One is Come," and the translation fits her well. A tall royal headpiece covers her hair. The profile beneath shows a high forehead extending down to form a straight nose, then full lips and a perfectly formed chin. It is the dark twinkling eyes, lined with black kohl to accentuate them, and the high cheek bones that mold the face into its final perfection. Her swan-like neck matches her thin flowing body.

Giggling sounds come from the garden.

"Ankhesenamun! You know you can hear me!"

Now she knows her mother means business. She doesn't call her by her full name unless she is being reprimanded or performing royal duties as a princess. The three run quickly toward the palace entrance.

Everyone knows the queen loves all of her children dearly, but Anie feels very special and knows that her mother relies on her the most. Her mother tells her that she is mature for her age, unlike her brother, Smenkhkare — whose name is fondly shortened to "Smenke." He is the oldest of the three siblings by a few years and should be the most responsible one, but he is not. Poor Smenke has wet the bed for many years, a fact the queen is still hiding from her husband, King Akhenaton. She knows that he would go into one of his famous rages if he knew about it. Smenke also likes to play and behave more like a girl. This concerns the queen and everyone else even more.

Physical beauty has passed by Anie's younger sister. Her lovely name Meritaten — "Meri"— doesn't seem to fit the girl. Her thin face is supported by a large hooked nose and she has a bad habit of whining through it when she doesn't get her way, which seems to be a lot of the time. Acting the fragile little creature, and aided by the look of helplessness, rescues her from many intolerable situations — to the dismay of Anie and Smenke. She also shows quite a stubborn streak at times, much like her father.

Glancing back, Anie sees her mother disappear from the balcony and enter her private quarters. The three race madly up the stone stairs, through the towering columns that support the covered front entrance, and enter the living room of the palace where the air is comfortably cool.

The adobe construction of the palace provides remarkable insulation properties, keeping the rooms pleasant during the day and warm when the nights turn cool. The climate is hot and dry most of the time. When the days become unbearably hot, an intricate water cooling system flows through clay pipes installed in walls and ceilings. And when warmth is needed, the system can be adjusted to allow the sun to collect and heat the water that runs through these same pipes.

Their running feet slide on the polished tile floors. Grabbing at the beautifully painted plastered walls they turn corners sharply. They know if they run fast enough to the covered walkway leading to their mother's quarters located in the private royal wing of the palace, they can surprise her before she has time to open her door to greet them.

Suddenly, a tall figure jumps out at them from the shadows.

"Boo!" a voice shouts.

All three jump and scream madly. When they see who it is, they are overjoyed. It is their half-brother.

Tutankhamun, fondly shortened to "Tut," is the unexpected guest. He lives in the palace at Memphis with grandmother Queen Tiyi, who is the widow of King Amenophis III and mother of Pharaoh Akhenaton.

At Memphis, Tut is obtaining the necessary education and instructions through private tutors to prepare him for possible future accession to the throne of Egypt. Royal blood flows through his veins.

Akhenaton, in a moment of passion and weakness,

had taken unto himself another wife two years after Anie was born. Their relationship was the source of much conflict and grief because Nefertiti could not accept such a betrayal of her affections, although it was perfectly legal by custom and tradition. The death of her rival, while giving birth to Tut, solved a most embarrassing and perplexing problem.

As the only mother Tut has ever known, Nefertiti occupies a special place in his heart. Likewise, Nefertiti looks upon Tut as an exceptional and loving son with all of the desirable qualities that her own son Smenke lacks.

Anie feels comfortable with her romantic inclinations toward Tut since he is not her full brother.

Even though Smenke is also receiving the special preparations, it is Tut who Nefertiti favors.

Everyone agrees that there is something special about Tut's personality and appearance. He has a way of pleasing everyone in a soft and polite manner. His five feet seven inch height makes him tower over most in this country where the people are shorter than he and of small stature. Like Anie, he is very mature for his age. With life expectancy of about forty years, he is already approaching manhood.

"Oh Tut, how wonderful to see you," sighs Anie. She gazes up into his brown eyes. They are interesting eyes – looking directly and deeply into hers – searching for secret thoughts. His thick, wavy dark brown hair almost covers his eyebrows. The remainder is clipped very short to accommodate the head pieces he must wear at royal ceremonies.

He bends down and gives her a warm kiss on the cheek. She blushes profusely. Meri and Smenke push in for their turns as they also love Tut. In the excitement they have forgotten all about their mother. Nefertiti can appear out of nowhere, it seems to them. Meri and Smenke want to go outside and play games, but Tut and Anie are less inclined to participate in the games the younger children enjoy. Holding hands, they see Nefertiti approaching.

Nefertiti explains about the morrow — a long day is planned that will take them to the banks of the Nile River — and a picnic.

The magic word picnic creates an air of excitement for Meri and Smenke. They are almost happy to obey her orders to go to bed early for a good night's rest. Tomorrow will be a fun day! Clapping their hands and chattering gleefully, they are whisked away to their own living quarters by the servants.

Tut squeezes Anie's hand gently and whispers, "until tomorrow."

2

JOURNEY TO THE BANKS OF THE NILE

After darkness of night ends and a new day is born, the Palace at Tell El Amarna emerges once again like a massive giant cradling its precious occupants.

Ankhesenamun awakens to the familiar sound of footsteps outside her bedroom door. A muffled "shush shush" noise is made on the hard tile floor as servants scurry back and forth in sandaled feet rushing to accomplish their many chores. The day begins early for them as there is much to do, not only the upkeep of the palace but their personal duties to perform for the royal family.

A covered walkway circles a small courtyard. The royal bedrooms, lining each side, face the luscious setting of green plants, small trees and lovely flowers. Chairs and small tables are placed in private nooks to offer moments of shared pleasure — leisure moments not often afforded to those in exalted positions. Schedules are filled with endless appointments. In the center of the courtyard a birdbath is provided for a group of feathered visitors who come daily to chirp happily, scold one another and, when no one is watching, indulge in a bath, splashing madly about until more water is needed to replenish their private pool. This is bird paradise.

Opening her eyes wide, Anie gazes about and a feeling of happiness and contentment spills over her. This room, her own special place, epitomizes the warmth and joy in her young life.

Reflecting off one of the copper shields placed strategically opposite an opening near the ceiling, the sun floods the room with welcome light. This opening is a clerestory type of window placed high up in the room and offers privacy. Its bars of carved stone keep out predators.

The walls are adorned with beautifully crafted tapestries and paintings. Outstanding art objects, meticulously created by gifted Egyptians, are arranged about the room. Some are huddled in niches in the walls. Elaborate furnishings include the hand-carved bedstead, chairs gilded and stacked with plump goose feather-filled pillows. Small tables and an array of gorgeous decorated chests hold the many necessities befitting a member of the royal family. All around there is gold — either painted or made of it.

As the princess snuggles under the linen sheets she hears a gentle tapping at the door. "Enter," she calls softly.

An attractive black girl only a few years older than she strolls into the room carrying a pile of fresh towels. "You remember, we are going on the picnic today." She is half telling and half reminding Anie.

The skin of the Nubian servant glows in the bright light and is as smooth as a baby's behind. Bold black eyes stare down at Anie. A wide smile reveals very straight teeth and their whiteness illuminates in contrast to her skin. As a small child she had been brought from a village in Nubia, a country located far to the south, and raised in the servants' quarters of the palace. Living in Nubia would have meant working in the gold mines and living a life filled with terrible working conditions. She knows how fortunate she is to be here.

The princess springs out of bed with her feet touching a soft woven mat that covers part of the beautifully tiled floor. Smiling and glowing with happiness she turns her young thin body in circles making the long sheer gown billow around her.

"Oh yes, Tahlia, prepare me — quickly!"

She darts across the room to her dressing table where a row of small finely-crafted ceramic pots and alabaster vases sit neatly in a row holding kohl— sticks for applying it — tweezers, hair curlers; in front of these are a comb and a bronze hand mirror. An intricately-carved small wooden cosmetic box holds malachite. There is a stone and palette for grinding cosmetics, a faience drinking cup and a lovely bronze bowl. On one side of the table are some breath-taking pieces of jewelry—gold rings and bracelets, a string of beads with an amulet, in the form of a scarab, hanging from it. Also, there is a large Egyptian collar into which hundreds of brilliantly-colored semi-precious stones have been hand-sewn.

Large, ornamented wood chests in assorted sizes and shapes are placed about the room holding everything imaginable for the adornment of this special person. They are elaborately carved and painted. On top of each chest Egyptian characters and symbols identify the contents.

Tahlia follows and carefully removes Ankhesenamun's sleeping garment and continues the personal duties as she is so well accustomed, leading her into the small connecting room, the lavatory. There she pours jugs of water into a basin and washes the delicate body. She removes the stopper in the basin and pours more water, flushing it out through the pipes that have been built into the walls and floors of the palace extending to an outside receptacle. After drying her with fine linen toweling, she assists her into the neatly prepared traveling clothes.

There is a closeness and devotion between the two young ladies. Tahlia knows her place as the servant — which is considered to be an honor if serving a member of the royal family. They delight in sharing their deepest secrets with one another and, most important, the princess knows that she can trust Tahlia.

"The Queen said that Prince Tutankhamun is coming today and is going with us." Tahlia is watching Ankhesenamun's reaction, knowing how fond the princess is of her half-brother.

"Oh, I'm so glad he is coming — it will make the day perfect!" She dances and whirls about the room.

There is much commotion throughout this wing of the palace with the numerous servants going in and out of the private quarters of the king and queen, the princesses and the princes. Breakfast is being delivered on large trays, chests are being packed and a multitude of last minute details are being attended — all for the comfort and pleasure of the royal family for their trip to the banks of the Nile. Even though the distance isn't of concern as it is not a long trip, safety is of the utmost concern. Protection of the royal family is of the essence.

"Tahlia, he's here!" Ankhesenamun races madly down the long hallway and, sliding around a corner, she finds herself gaping up at Tutankhamun. She feels that same wonderful emotion inside her again whenever she is near him. It is always the same.

"Oh, Tut, are you ready to go?" she asks breathlessly.

Now it is his turn to let her know how pleased he is to see her. Staring down at her he drinks in her exquisite beauty and notes that it is not the classic type of her mother but the roundness and softness of a young lady. Hazel-colored eyes are fringed with heavy black lashes and perfectly carved thick eyebrows. Her long black wavy hair hangs thickly and gracefully down her back, ending at a tiny waist. The flawless olive-colored skin is like her mother's, but the mouth is fuller with lips that need no artificial coloring. When she smiles, dimples appear in the unblemished cheeks.

With the strict learning schedule Tut has to adhere to day after day — always being reminded that he must study hard for his preparation as a king — to be with Anie even for a short time is a thrill for him. She is two years older than he, but the age difference is neither noticeable nor important.

He takes her hand in his and they run laughing and talking to the awaiting caravan.

Single file, the troop of Nubian slaves walks happily along the narrow road, some carrying the covered canopies holding the royal family, some shouldering the supplies while others coax the animals on their way.

The delicate fragrance from blossoms of the sweet acacia trees fill the air. A sycamore tree bows its head. Cotton fields are in abundance as well as wheat fields and they seem to beckon their welcome by waving to and fro like graceful dancers keeping in rhythm with the ever-so-soft breeze. Occasional groves of date palms and fig trees lend their contribution of food and beauty.

But it is the demarcation line vividly drawn separating green lushness and sand that is truly remarkable. Not even a blade of grass is allowed to cross over into what seems to be the forbidden vastness of sandy hills in the great desert. As infinite oceans churn on forever to meet the endless sky, so does the desert roll on and on until it too meets the sky.

Two long, sturdy poles have been attached to a wooden structure consisting of a floor and a double seat. There are small poles that reach upward to support a curtained enclosure.

Four slaves hoist the carrier on their strong shoulders, using the long poles for support.

As the carrier with Ankhesenamun and Tahlia makes its way down a wide dirt road, they are enjoying the jostled ride while peering through the filmy curtains that enclose them. People living in the small villages wave and chant welcome greetings. Parting the curtain and leaning out slightly, the princess waves to a man working in the fields. He is using his mihrath, a typical Egyptian plow consisting of a wooden pole six feet long with a metal-tipped stake at the rear to make a shallow furrow. It is drawn by two oxen. Using a wooden pitchfork, another man is winnowing wheat — pitching grain and light chaff up into the air to be separated by the wind. Peasants like these toil from dawn to dusk with only a midday rest when the searing sun becomes too hot to bear.

Women work in the fields also, especially at harvest time. Some are seen carrying clay jugs on top of their heads, walking with confidence and ease. They have just returned from the edge of the Nile where they have filled them with water. Crocodiles keep their distance, for now. Lying on nearby shores — territory they demand for themselves — they slither out into the murky water when their stomachs become empty. Even though they are worshiped as a god at one of the villages, the peasants keep their distance as they do not want to become a meal for one of them. Fortunately, crocodiles are few in this particular region because of the dense populace that disturbs them. It is at Elephantine Island, far to the south, where there are few inhabitants that the creatures are more dangerous and plentiful.

A young girl wades out into the dirty water and bends down for a drink. She pushes debris away and skims some water up into her cupped hand. The debris contains a dead fish or two. Long usage of this polluted water has brought about bodily accommodation and acceptance that foreign visitors find hard to understand. Troublesome diarrhea is their usual payment for drinking this water.

On each side of the Nile are small villages and towns. Rows and rows of little mud huts can be seen nestled along the banks of the river. These represent inhabitants of the lower end of the economic scale.

Ankhesenamun can't help noticing a special look in the eyes of the villagers. It is a look of inner contentment and peace. Their faces seem to glow as they smile at her. A very elderly man is sitting cross-legged at the entrance of his hut where he has found a nice shady spot. A broad, toothless smile spreads slowly and evenly over his wrinkled face. A white turban graces his head, and a loin cloth is wrapped around his hips. This is the popular garb worn by the peasants.

The Egyptians are a good looking people. For the most part, they are small in stature, small-boned, olive-skinned, medium to dark colored hair and usually have dark brown eyes. Most are very thin and their skin is tanned from the merciless desert sun.

"Remember, your highness, do not give the children any trinkets or food. It is dangerous to do so." Tahlia is sitting close to the princess and is worrying to herself. She knows how generous and unknowing the princess can be.

"But the children are so thin — and those horrible flies are everywhere!" sighs Ankhesenamun in her quiet way.

The flies are bold and sticky, making themselves ever present, even on the faces of the young children and babies. They crawl over and around their eyes, noses and mouths, knowing they have gained control of the situation. It is as if the people have given up trying to discourage the insidious pests. As a baby laughs, the flies enter triumphantly at the corners of the toothless open smiling mouth.

The caravan has just marched around a corner and is easing itself slowly along a wide dirt road. On either side there is a sharp slope obliterating everything below. Suddenly, and without warning, the carrier containing Ankhesenamun and Tahlia is completely surrounded by screaming children. They have come in droves up and over the high banks to the carrier. In a frenzy they are reaching, pulling and grabbing through the curtains at the frightened occupants.

"I warned you!" Tahlia shouts angrily as she tries to fight off the mass of scratching and clawing hands. She suspects that Ankhesenamun gave something to one of the children earlier, when she was not looking. Tahlia knows that as soon as one child receives something the word spreads quickly and then they all want something. It is not a vicious act by any means but a natural one; just wanting anything available. They do not wish to physically hurt the princess — she is simply a victim of mob reaction.

"I didn't mean to, Tahlia!" she sobs. "Stop, stop! Keep away!" Knowing she has blundered, she pushes the clawing hands from her.

Seeing what is happening, the carrier just behind stops abruptly and Tutankhamun and Smenkhkare alight and run hurriedly to the frenzied group. With the help of the slaves and the guards they quickly push and coax the excited children away.

"Are you all right?" Tut asks affectionately. He is aware of what has happened and is ready to scold her, but as he parts the torn curtain and sees the tear-stained face and wide frightened eyes, he knows a lesson has been learned the hard way and no further rebuking is necessary. Anie is so happy to see him. She reaches out and draws him close to her while her heart pounds with fright. As she rests her chin on his shoulder, she feels the warm embrace of his gentle arms envelop her. Further words are not necessary.

As everyone returns to their appointed positions, the caravan continues on its journey, winding its way along more dusty roads at a snail's pace and finally stops at a pre-designated picnic area. The corn flowers and blue lotus along the Nile banks seem to be looking up at them with their beautiful flower-faces as if they are letting them know they are pleased they have come.

As the carriers are set down there is a mad scramble for favorite picnic spots. Food and supplies are readily prepared. Everyone indulges until they can eat and drink no more and then seek quiet resting places.

Tut grabs Anie's hand in his and, waving farewell to the others, they run off to their favorite place among the tall grass. Yellow daisies, poppies and irises are abundant. But it is the blue lotus floating at the water's edge — a plant of the water lily family — that attracts their attention. He stoops down and plucks one of the gems and places it carefully in her hands. The flower has an almost weightless feeling.

"The blue lotus represents the Nile — giver and sustainer of life," he whispers softly in her ear. "This is for you, Anie." He gazes lovingly down into the anxious eyes.

"You are my flower of the Nile."

The magic moment is broken by a voice in the distance.

"Hurry children, we must be on our way!" Nefertiti is waving to Meri and Smenke. "And find Anie and Tut." She knows it will take the long caravan a while to make its way down the road to a small village where their royal visit is eagerly awaited. As she is helped into her plush carrier, her narrow buttocks sink down into the soft pillows that have been placed in a neat row for her comfort. She glances back and sees the four of them running happily to their proper places in the line. How she envies their young energy. She feels very blessed to be a part of this happy family and gives a soft murmur of thankful prayer to one of her favorite gods. She is sorry that Akhenaton could not be with them on this short trip, but she knows his royal duties as Pharaoh of all Egypt prevents him from accompanying them very often. Even though they have been having many quarrels recently about their extremely different religious beliefs, she loves and misses him.

The caravan leaves the green fields and slowly edges its way up the narrow hot road into the desert. Sand is everywhere. The earth looks like it is now completely consumed by it. Hills are humped in soft mounds and their unscathed surfaces gleam in the bright sunlight. As they follow a bend in the road, little adobe huts suddenly appear snugly nestled along the side of one of the great sand hills — its strange formation protecting them like large spread arms. The villagers begin to appear, not only from the mouths of the huts but from everywhere — as if the giant hills of sand are belching them from their fat bellies.

The greeters are mostly young women, children and old people since the men of the households are either laboring in the nearby fields or are taking their honored turn working on a temple or tomb for the Pharaoh.

Occasionally a friendly goose makes its unexpected appearance and sounds a honk of welcome.

As the caravan marches into its appointed place the villagers rush forward to see the royal family. Nefertiti does her job well as official hostess, smiling and waving at all who can get close to her — as close as the guards will allow. They keep an ever-watchful eye on the situation. The princesses and princes also show they have practiced well their royal lessons. Good manners and proper etiquette are displayed.

After the preliminaries, from the corner of her eye, Nefertiti sees Anie and Tut running off together. The guards are busy watching the Queen so they do not see them. She knows it would be to no avail if she did try to call them back. They would probably act like they could not hear her. After all, why shouldn't they have some fun of their own, she tells herself. She sees them disappear from sight over one of the sandy knolls.

The people are enjoying themselves. Small groups form and lively conversation ensues.

All of a sudden, muffled screams can be heard in the distance. A hush falls over the crowd.

"Mastaba! Mastaba!" yells a terrified villager as he comes running up from the same hill that Anie and Tut had gone over.

A feeling of fear sweeps over Nefertiti and her heart begins to pound harder and harder.

"Where are Tut and Anie?" she screams frantically.

"They have fallen into the mastaba," groans the informer.

A large woman jumps forward. "We must act quickly — there is no time to lose!" She motions to a group behind her and they start running towards the hill as fast as they can. Their bare feet sink into the deep sand making it difficult to move fast in the stubborn folds of grainy particles.

Smenke and Meri join the group in hot pursuit. Smenke is crying and Meri is wide-eyed with fright.

Excavation work has been going on at this mastaba near the village for some time and temporary wooden planks have been laid over the top of the opening. The soft winds of the desert have blown thin layers of sand over the planks, hiding them from view. Sloping sides underneath lead deeply down into the tomb.

These mastabas were the first type of burial places for the nobles and kings of Egypt – forerunners of the pyramids. They were made of mud, brick or stone, flat-topped, rectangular in shape with a shaft descending to the burial chamber far below.

A mastaba could have a few or as many as thirty rooms. Usually the story of the deceased and his family was painted on plastered walls. Their daily life, celebrations, scenes of vineyards, wheat fields, herds of cattle, jugs of wine and even love-making were revealed on the walls.

Some tombs had a sealed "false" door which was slightly recessed and located at the end of one of the rooms. This particular door was to enable the Ka, or spirit of the deceased, to enter the main part of the tomb and partake of the food and use the comforts left for it.

Hallways that lead from the main room to the burial chamber could have religious inscriptions on the walls to help the deceased meet the requirements for their afterlife.

These mastabas, like other kinds of Egyptian burial places, were emptied by robbers. This mastaba was no exception. People of the small village had found the usual empty mastaba. Its contents had been emptied many years before — probably when it was freshly finished.

Hand in hand, Anie and Tut had been happily running to find a secluded place, just wanting to be together — away from other people.

There was no warning! It was a sudden shock to both of them and they could feel their feet give way beneath them. The earth had opened up and was sucking them downward. Helplessly, they were being drawn into the deep shaft that lead into the mastaba. The loose sand poured quickly onto their crumpled bodies, trying to create a sandy grave. The sand covered them completely as if to embrace them in its fatal hold forever.

In one quick movement, as they were plunging downward, Tut flung his body over Anie's. The silent sand covered them in darkness. The only opening was a small air pocket Tut had been able to make with his face against Anie's.

Anie could feel the heavy weight of Tut on top of her and the sand engulfing her very being. She tried to keep her eyes and mouth tightly closed, and tried not to breathe, hoping her lungs could endure the struggle of life and death. She could feel Tut's weak breath pushing against her nose. She knew he was trying to share some air with her. There was not much to share.

"Please find us and help us!" she thinks to herself. Then blackness engulfs her and she dreams of being in a dark windowless room.

Tut feels her body go limp beneath him and terror fills his heart.

"Oh hurry, hurry—please!" he pleads. And then the black hand of unconsciousness waved its power over him.

"Dig! Dig! Faster! Faster!" scream Smenke and Meri in unison as the villagers keep scooping up sand in their now bleeding hands. The hidden rocks are cutting and tearing at their soft flesh. Frantic cries keep erupting from the Queen as she envisions their impending death.

Time seems to move slowly.

Then a piercing cry of, "I've reached them!" cuts through the mute crowd.

The form of a body appears in the sandy grave. Sand is quickly pushed away and Tut's limp body is lifted promptly up and out of the hole and laid on the ground. Then Anie is pulled up gently and placed beside him. Two villagers lean down, one over Tut and the other over Anie, and breathe air into each of their mouths. All is silent. Then, from the two ashen faces, eyes flutter and life reappears.

A groan of thankfulness sweeps over the entire crowd with the realization that the children will be all right. A look of loving relief shows on the faces of Nefertiti, Smenke and Meri.

It is a happy and tired caravan that winds its way back to the great palace at Tell El Amarna.

3

EGYPTIAN RELIGION

Another beautiful day is beginning in the land of enchanting Egypt as the sun settles a bright kiss on the heads of two people enjoying their breakfast together on one of the large verandas of the palace. The newly scrubbed wet floor reflects the sun's rays like twinkling dew drops.

The King and Queen of Egypt are being served and pampered by the numerous servants — some are Egyptians and some are Nubians. Bustling about, they attend to every whim of the royal couple. The service rendered is one of love, not contempt, since the Pharaoh is worshiped as a god. Even the black Nubian slaves, who are prizes from the terrible wars in the south, work contentedly and faithfully. The smell of freshly baked bread fills the air and second portions are served from one of the gold trays. Gestures of genuine caring is evident.

This caring and worship of a Pharaoh as a god-like person began hundreds of years before with King Narmer, also known as Menes, who united Upper and Lower Egypt. So the worship of Akhenaton as Pharaoh of all Egypt is justified by his birthright and royal accession to the throne.

Ingrained in them from birth, the people of Egypt are deeply engrossed in their religious beliefs. They try to live a good life on earth, and believe this same good life will continue in the afterlife. But their godlike Pharaoh is thought to continue his existence in the world of the stars in his afterlife, ascending to heaven to be with the gods. The Pharaoh is imagined as joining the Sun-god Ra and traveling with him in his solar boat through the sky by day and then in another boat through the perilous darkness of the underworld by night. He is protected by magical formulae which are inscribed on the walls of his tomb. To be sure this needed transportation is available, a solar boat is buried near his tomb.

Nefertiti's religion dates back to primitive times and, now in this "New Empire" era, is practiced by her and most of the people. The Egyptians are so indoctrinated in it that change of any kind is unheard of. They never give up the worship of numerous old gods — they just add on to them, making their religion more complicated than ever.

This religion is of an animistic nature, the doctrine that the phenomena of animal life is produced by a soul, or spiritual force, distinct from matter.

All along the Nile Valley in each village and in various districts of the Delta there is the belief that a guardian spirit dwells in some animal, bird, reptile, tree or plant special to that village which plays a prominent part in the life of that particular locality. It is considered either to be life-giving and friendly — or menacing. Whichever the case, the favor of the guardian spirit has to be solicited with set words and actions, with appropriate offerings and a private dwelling in which to reside. This dwelling, or temple, is staffed by local priests to take care of the god's daily needs. In return for these services the god protects the people, insures the fertility of their fields and herds and sees to their well-being. If the god is not cared for he can pour his wrath upon them in the form of plague, famine or other terrible disaster.

The worship of animals has become more and more popular as evidenced by Anubis of Kynopolis, a dog or jackal-god associated with the cult of the dead and mummification. Another is Sebek, the crocodile-god worshiped in Crocodilopolis. Taweret, the hippopotamus goddess, is especially worshiped by women during pregnancy. The lion-goddess is Sekhmet, meaning "Powerful One," and the cat-goddess is Bast. There is Wepwawet, the "opener of the ways," and Khentiamentiu who presides over the desert of the west, an early god of Abydos who later became merged with Osiris.

Birds, understandably, occupy a unique position as sky-gods. Especially prominent are hawks or falcons. The Sun-god Ra himself is always depicted as hawk-headed. Horus the hawk, the ancient Sky-god of Hierakonopolis is the one that the king is thought to mount and fly up to heaven at his death.

In previous years when the bull gods — such as Apis, Mnevis and Buchis — died they were mummified and put in a stone sarcophagus. A search was then made for a calf born at the time of death in which the god might have been reincarnated. And now, in later times, the mummification of other animals is the custom, burying them in special cemeteries or catacombs at Abydos, Hermopolis, Crocodilopolis, Elephantine and other places. The whole species is regarded as sacred.

Development of religion has followed closely the political development of the country. The success of a ruler in a small village can have an effect on the god worshiped there. The god can get more influential in a larger place and finally achieve national status when its worship becomes the state cult. Such happened with Amun of Thebes when he became "king of the gods" at this time — and Nefertiti's belief.

For centuries the ancient Egyptians never developed any tendency toward the worship of one god. Now, Akhenaton and his handful of followers, mostly priests, prefer the sun disk Aton above all other gods. They even resort to the destruction of sacred images. This has caused friction between the King and the Queen as well as serious dissension among the people. It is also very difficult for the offspring of the royal couple. The children are being torn between their parents' religious beliefs — trying to please both.

Akhenaton's deceased father was King Amenhotep III, and his widow, Queen Tiyi, is Akenaton's mother. Pharaoh Akenaton tries to be a good husband and exhibits a genuine caring for his wife and children most of the time. But he is indeed a rebellious king.

"I'm glad yesterday is over," says Nefertiti.

"You should have the children watched more closely," Akhenaton adds, glaring directly into her eyes.

"And where were all the guards?"

She leans over and glares angrily in return.

"If you weren't always so busy with your obsession to change the religion of the whole country and send armies of men to kill people in foreign countries you just might have some time to help supervise the protection of the children."

After her outburst she settles back comfortably in her chair, feeling a little ashamed of her accusations. After all, he is so good to her in many ways. As she sits watching him devour the well-cooked scrambled pigeon eggs — chewing with mouthfuls of pleasure — she can't help but be engrossed by his physical appearance. He is certainly lacking in any good-looking qualities, with his pot-belly sticking out roundly beneath his robe. The elongated skull and womanish features certainly rule out any handsome traits. But she enjoys his lovemaking and finds no cause to complain about that.

"I know, my dear," he says softly, patting her hand. "You are correct and I am sorry, but as Pharaoh my duties to the country must come first at all times. I know that I am responsible for introducing this new religion, but I sincerely believe in Aton, whose symbol is the sun. I do not actually worship the sun itself but simply a universal power — a bringing of light and life — the power beyond the sun."

He continues: "And as for the wars, it is my responsibility to see that Egypt is defended from foreign intruders, and if that means killing the innocent, then that is the tragic result of all wars."

As Nefertiti sits listening she begins feeling more and more ashamed of herself. She realizes how fortunate she is to sit on the throne beside him. She is allowed to do almost anything she cares to do — anything but having a say about how the country should be ruled. She knows there is no stopping his insistence on changing the Amun religion to his beloved Aton. Also, she believes that in his heart he wants to build a great Egyptian empire.

The sound of children running in the hallway ends their conversation. The bright and babbling faces of Anie, Meri and Smenke appear. They dash to the loving arms of their parents. These are the times when the Queen misses Tut. How she wishes he could be with them. But she keeps reminding herself that he must be with the Queen Mother Tiyi at her palace to continue his royal studies. There is no other way.

"I'm going to have the artist come and paint our family portrait," bellows Akhenaton. "Then it can be chiseled on the walls of one of the temples for all to see."

Nefertiti nods in agreement. She knows that he is the first Pharaoh to seem human to the people of Egypt and something like this portrait has not been attempted before. As he instructs a servant to carry out his wishes, Nefertiti gazes at the small group around her reluctantly. She admits to herself that the children are maturing into young adults. Anie, she observes closely, is beginning her physical development with her small breasts starting to fill the hollows of her garment. She has already come to her mother questioning the unusual discharge of blood from her body. Nefertiti has explained to her daughter that this is not unusual and that she will have this womanly occurrence about every twenty-eight days and it will last for about three to six days. She also instructs her to keep a record on her calendar.

The calendar has always intrigued Anie and she has paid special attention to her private tutor when it had been explained to her. It is interesting to her that the Egyptian calendar had been introduced hundreds of years before, and lately additional investigation has been done and some changes made. By now the day and the night are each divided into twelve hours, but since the day is measured sometimes from sunrise to sunset and sometimes from the appearance of daylight to its disappearance, the length of day and of night vary throughout the year.

Her tutor had explained that in earlier years they had begun to observe the heliacal rising – the risings and settings of the stars that take place as near the sun as they can be observed – of the star Sirius, a conspicuous object in the Egyptian sky. They had noted that the rising corresponded very closely with the flooding of the Nile, on which agricultural welfare of the country depended. They chose this for the first day of the year and took the period between two such observed risings to form a unit of time which was convenient not only as being much longer than the old month, but as including a complete cycle of the season.

In the next step, they subdivided the new unit, making use of both the old months and of the changing seasons. Twelve nominal months of thirty days each equaled 360 days, and the missing five days were added on at the end under the name of "days additional to the year." The months were grouped into three sets of four — inundation season, winter, or sow-time, and summer, or harvest time.

The months bear no special names, written merely as the first, second, third or fourth month of such and such a season. Anie marks her calendar accordingly.

As Nefertiti finishes her instructions to her daughter she finds herself observing her husband once again. She is truly sorry that the domestic quarrels about religion have become so heated between them

— and so often of late. She feels at times that they are growing further and further apart. There are indications that he is not thinking clearly — as if he disappears mentally. But she keeps telling herself that it is only her imagination. After all, he is the Pharaoh — a god. He is perfect.

But this instant, for the first time, she notices an odd look in Akhenaton's eyes when he is looking at Anie. The Queen senses that it is not a fatherly glance but one filled with lust. It can't be, she assures herself.

Shouts of, "Grandfather is here!" interrupts her concentration. A welcome figure stands in the doorway. He is handsome with finely cut facial features. The three excited children run to him smothering him with hugs and kisses and almost knocking off the headpiece perched high on his head. As he bows down to embrace each one he says, "Ankhesenamun, Smenkhkare, Meritaten." A sound of pride is detected in the soft voice. Deep-set kindly-looking eyes peer through dark brown irises flecked with gray. They twinkle now as he observes his grandchildren. Gathering his wits about him he stands erect and carefully straightens the blue flowing robe that covers his long lean body. Sandaled feet are hidden beneath the deep folds.

"Father! How wonderful to see you!" Nefertiti runs forward and gives him a big hug. The family resemblance is strongly evident.

Akhenaton raises his right hand in salutation: "Ay, it is nice to see you."

Ay is the High Priest now during Akhenaton's reign. In this New Empire era of Egyptian history the priests play an integral part.

Since religion dominates all the people of the land, there is a need for many priests. The priesthood is usually passed from father to son, and ranks from the most humble to the High Priest.

In previous years the Egyptian monarch was empowered to exercise priestly functions before all the gods, but now the professional priests have attained enormous power. They are exempt from paying taxes and are not required to lend their servants to till the fields or to haul the quarried stones for construction work at the great palaces and temples. No portion of yield from their lands is expected in tribute. They increase in number so rapidly — an average temple has a staff of twenty to fifty and the large national temple has many thousands of priests — they have to be divided in special units. The temples possess larger and larger estates and become increasingly more and more wealthy. High Priest Ay controls one of the greatest land holdings in Egypt, consisting of nearly thirty percent of all the arable land. His power is second only to the Pharaoh.

The priesthood is called "we'eb" meaning "pure" and bodily purity is ensured by ablution, washing the mouth with natron and shaving all hair from the head, face and body including the eyebrows and eyelashes.

As the years have passed, Ay no longer follows the strict adherence to all the bodily shaving. He prefers to keep his eyelashes and a head of hair that is cut very short so it cannot be seen when he wears the tall headpiece. His exalted position allows for some preference, but his is expected to remain a good example to all the other priests — especially the young ones. He does practice and keep other priestly beliefs such as not eating the flesh of local cult animals, and abstaining from sexual relations with women.

When Ay was very young, and before taking his final vows, he met and fell in love with a beautiful young princess. Nefertiti was born of that union. The princess was banished — never to be heard from again. A brokenhearted Ay had to leave the rearing of his child in the hands of others behind palace walls. Authoritative priests at that time granted forgiveness of his sin only if he would swear not to have sexual relations with any other women for the remainder of his life. He agreed and has kept his word. Through the many years, honor and respect have been earned by this genuinely caring man.

As Ay stands before Akhenaton, he is a picture of dignity. He prefers to wear a long robe rather than the usual brief white linen wrapped around the loins — the standard uniform for priests.

"Your Highness, I must inform you of the mounting tension derived from your Aton cult and implore you to re-think your position. The growing religious debate is becoming more serious each day." Ay's persuasive voice booms out.

"Don't be ridiculous!" shouts the king. "I intend to follow this through to the bitter end if necessary."

"It will be to your end," retorts Ay, holding his ground but with an added authoritative softness that has been taught and drilled into him in his rigorous priesthood training. "I must also inform you of the latest events of the war. All is not well in Syria and Palestine. The Hittites are beginning to invade the principalities of northern Syria, while invaders from the Eastern desert are fighting for our possessions in

Palestine. Many hundreds of lives are being lost, not to mention the wounded, numbering in the thousands."

"You are over-reacting!" The king begins to ramble on in a slow rage. "Our professional army is at my command. The infantry is trained and disciplined to fight on every kind of terrain — and from ships, if necessary. And don't forget our chariot troops. Those horses can run down the invaders very effectively."

Nefertiti senses it is time to end the fruitless debate. "Can you stay for dinner, father?" she asks with a plea in her voice.

"No, my dear, I must return to the temple now."

The grandchildren, bored with the adult conversation, had returned to the garden and now wave and throw kisses to him.

Pleased with his outburst, Akhenaton settles back in his chair and waves a half-hearted farewell. Food is more important to him now.

As Ay and Nefertiti walk closely together down the wide hallway and with no one to overhear their conversation, she pours her feelings of despair on her father's patient ear. It is not only the religion that is tearing her apart from her husband, she tells her father, but it is recent suspicion of Akhenaton's growing abnormal sexual interest in Ankhesenamun.

Giving his daughter a fatherly embrace, he tries to assure her that it cannot be true. "Let's hope you are just imagining this — there is probably nothing to it at all."

Nefertiti watches her father as he descends the stone steps, throwing a goodbye kiss to her.

He is not very convincing, not even to himself.

4

ANWAR

The Queen's quarters are beautiful. A large balcony, with colorful gardens nestled beneath, extends out from the spacious rooms and is situated to catch the cool evening breezes and to offer many hours of relaxing pleasure. As in the other rooms of the royal family the furniture and decorations are something to marvel. In one area of the bedroom a wooden bedstead is flanked by two gilded chairs. Its legs end with carved animal paws and two of the four corner posts have elaborately carved animal heads, painted black. Their brightly-colored, all-seeing eyes peer menacingly about the room as if seeking unwanted intruders.

Multi-colored reed mats hang loosely on the plastered walls; remarkable objects crafted in gold, and mirrors made of bronze hang between them, glistening and reflecting in the polished tile floor.

The bathroom leading off the bedroom has a quartzite wash basin placed in a hollowed-out counter. A painted wooden toilet box sits in a corner with a round hole cut out in the seat. After use, jugs of water are poured and forced down into it to wash the waste material away in large clay pipes leading from the building. The slave with least seniority has the duty of disposing of this foul smelling material.

"Come in children," Nefertiti calls as she lovingly gestures towards the trio. "How would you like to make a pilgrimage on the royal yacht down the Nile to see the Pyramids?" Anxiously she awaits their reaction. It's a long trip of 450 miles and of several days duration. She knows they would have to leave very soon to complete the trip before the first month of harvest. After that, the heat becomes intense and the fierce winds that follow create horrible dust storms.

"Yes, yes! We want to go!" They all chime together like ringing bells.

"Can Tut go too?" Anie asks quickly while searching her mother's face for confirmation.

"No," replies her mother, "He must stay at Grandmother Tiyi's and study." She notes a look of disappointment.

A frenzied three days later all is in readiness for the long trip. The usual caravan assembles at the gates of the palace and the trek on the dusty road begins. Winding and maneuvering as before, they travel down the serpentine road that leads to the banks of the Nile. At the river's edge barges and boats are already being loaded with furnishings and supplies.

The large royal yacht stands patiently awaiting its human cargo. Passengers are assisted in walking the wide wooden plank that leads onto the deck. Anie, Meri and Smenke hang over the sides and watch the servants and slaves carry the bundles of supplies up the adjacent gang-plank.

When all is in readiness the yacht is untied and pushed from the muddy shore. It is 200 feet long, and the rigging is made of papyrus. The large sail, made of Egyptian cotton, is billowing in the soft breeze like a huge giant taking puffs of needed air. It moves slowly and majestically down the river.

Anie waves to the well-wishers lined along the shore. Some are women carrying water jugs on top of their heads and some are children gaily running and laughing and waving back. Some are using the river for bathing and others are doing their laundering. Men plowing in their fields and canal diggers stop for a moment to return her welcome greeting. These are the same shores that she and Tut enjoy so much together. Blue lotus flowers float at the river's edge and beautiful swaying palm trees reach toward the sky. "I miss him so much," she sighs to herself.

The two collapsible canopies, used for the royal family's comfort on long trips into the desert and on trips such as this one from Thebes to Giza, had earlier been brought on board and erected on the deck, side by side. The structures are ingeniously made with copper-sheathed mortise-and-tendon joints for rapid dismantling and re-erection — and spacious — each ten feet long, eight feet wide and seven feet high. The tent-like framework of beams and posts is made of wood painted gold. Curtains cover the roof and hang down on three sides with a split set drawn across the front used for the entrance. Results are a very comfortable enclosed room suitable for the mild climate in Egypt at this season of the year.

A familiar face suddenly emerges from behind the curtained opening, followed by another welcome surprise.

Anie's face lights up with joy. "We were told you couldn't come, Tut." She is laughing as she makes her way towards him. "And Grandmother Tiyi — how wonderful to see you too!" Warm hugs and embraces are shared by all as the other members of the royal family come to see what all the excitement is about. Nefertiti looks puzzled by the change of plans. "I thought Tut was supposed to stay with you and study." "He does indeed," replies Tiyi. Pulling back the curtain she adds: "And here is another pleasant surprise for all of you."

A shadowy figure in the background of the tent steps forward. He is tall like Tut, but a few years older. The added years have produced a more mature physique with broad shoulders and well-developed muscles — all in the right places. Black wavy hair frames a handsome face. Dark eyes are twinkling and dancing with amusement. He knows that the children will not want him to be here.

Tiyi takes his arm and draws him close to her. "Anwar has been invited to join us with the understanding that his tutoring skills shall be used here on the yacht for the children. Tutankhamun – she always addresses her grand-children by their full names and is not likely to change – will continue his studies as well as the others. They will all have advantage of this splendid opportunity."

The children sigh and groan in discontentment, but Nefertiti agrees. She knows only too well that after a while they will become bored. This will be a good outlet for them and especially with such a fine tutor as Anwar.

Anwar had previously been a scribe. He was born in one of the small villages, and at the age of five started a twelve-year study program to become a scribe. During those twelve years he had to write all day, using a brush and ink, writing on papyrus — sometimes on a wooden board or piece of broken pottery — practicing hieroglyphs over and over again. And not only did he study that art, but also arithmetic, geography, history and had some instruction on the complex structure of the government and the temples.

Thousands of scribes are used and needed since tax records are kept on such things as harvests of the farmers, number of fish caught by the fisherman, inventories of artists, and on and on. Taxes are paid in produce, livestock and labor. Census records are kept on every man, woman and child and all domestic animals. Even lists of customs duties received at country entry posts are kept by the scribes. The army and the priests use them for keeping all kinds of records of recruits, supplies and secretarial services — writing important letters and keeping detailed accounts of all this. Anwar has even written a book on his own, but now he has been promoted to this position of very high esteem, that of private tutor for the royal family.

"As soon as everyone is settled we shall begin our first lesson." Anwar feels overjoyed at this great opportunity, not only to teach but to be included on this special trip. He welcomes a repeat trip to the great pyramids.

Anie, Meri, Smenke and Tut all groan in unison.

"That's enough!" "You are all to do as Anwar says." It is their mother's voice letting them know she means what she says. They know better than to disobey her wishes. Off they go for their hour of reprieve.

The four run to one side of the magnificent yacht and, with torsos and necks outstretched, they lean over the railing to see the bustling activities abounding on the water. Large barges are going up and down the river, some carrying cargoes of grain, some stacked high with bundles of reeds, and still others laden with neat piles of clay jugs. With their sails swelling, the swift and light feluccas are performing their ferry duties, adding picturesque silhouettes. Little barges are lined up in front of their appointed places to be ready at any time for their towing duties. But it is the majestic and colorful royal yacht that is the beauty to behold. Its hull, made of short wooden planks, laid up like bricks in a wall, doweled together and edge-fastened place construction, looks like a fine piece of hand-rubbed varnished furniture. The extended bow is decorated with a carved likeness of a snarling leopard awaiting its prey.

The passengers are dressed in gorgeous gowns and gold-covered headpieces. Multi-colored and jeweled wide collars, priceless body ornaments made of gold and silver and precious stones, sparkling in the sunlight, complete the extravagant picture.

"It's time for your lessons," Anwar calls.

The children don't move.

"I know it's difficult to have to come in now and have a lesson but it is part of your learning and training."

Unhappily, they do Anwar's bidding and make their way slowly into one of the sheltered canopies protecting them from the heat and flies. Sliding into their assigned chairs that have been placed neatly in a row each is given a pen, a small bottle of ink and papyrus on which to write.

"Since we are going to see the great pyramids at Giza, I thought a short history lesson about them and the Nile River would be in order for today." Anwar stands confidently before them and continues:

"Our ancestors, living along the Nile before the Great Pyramids were built, were agricultural people and herdsmen. They domesticated the animals that we enjoy today.".

"King Narmer unified Upper and Lower Egypt about eighteen hundred years ago, and most of our history is identified from his reign."

"About four hundred and fifty years later, King Zoser's Step Pyramid and Temple at Saqqarah were the first buildings to be actually built entirely of stone. It was the king's chief architect, Imhotep, a writer and physician, who designed this elaborate complex of stone buildings, courts and chapels, decorated with limestone, covering an area of 180,000 square yards and exhibiting amazing artistry in design and craftsmanship. The creative skills of stone cutters and sculptors were called into play to give the appearance of log ceilings, and reed matted walls to the lifeless stone. Huge stone columns, with fluted plant-like tops, supported the massive ceilings."

"The Step Pyramid was actually six mastabas set one on top of the other, the small blocks of stone laid together like bricks. It is mammoth in size — 413 by 344 feet at the base and 200 feet high — and we are informed that it has underground chambers."

"After that, pyramids were built at Dashur, Maydum, Abu Roash and Giza. We will see the three Great Pyramids at Giza."

"And now some information about the Nile." Anwar glances about him to make sure his students have not fallen asleep.

"Without the Nile we cannot exist. As you can see, our great river is perfect for transportation and communication. But it is also life-giving as it rises in the inundation season to flood and fertilize the fields. Torrential rains in Ethiopia rush northward and the lowlands become covered, with only higher towns remaining above water."

"The river even approaches the Great Pyramids of Giza."

"Then it subsides for the winter when the crops grow in abundance in the black, rich soil that is deposited. When the season is dry, water is drawn from the low Nile channel."

"Those unfortunate ones who chose to build on lower ground experience the full ravages of the river during the wet seasons. The dikes we have built in some areas have helped. And, of course, it can be the other way also, with too little water and resultant lack of food."

"The construction of large catchment basins help trap needed water in the wet season. Canals leading from these to the fields insure a more dependable and controlled inundation. High water poles are used to measure the rise of the river."

"The papyrus on which you are writing is from the Nile's edge. The tall papyrus reed grows thickly in the swamps of the Delta. The fibers of the plant, when twisted, make our ropes. The sandals you are wearing are made from papyrus; mats, baskets, stools, boxes and many other things are made from this useful plant. Even our small boats are made from bundles of bound papyrus reeds."

"Now, that wasn't so bad, was it?" Anwar asks as he concludes his talk, hoping he has enlightened them — maybe just a little.

Yawning, the children leave the comfortable enclosure. Obvious sighs of relief can be heard.

5

PYRAMIDS AND THE SPHINX

The large boat glides silently through the Nile like an ominous slithering crocodile after its unsuspecting prey. Steered by a large bladed oar situated in the stern, and assisted by wind from the south, the craft is only slightly affected. Sailing conditions are perfect.

The welcome silence is broken by shouts of, "We're here!"

The bustle of activity begins like the sound of angry bees. Sharp commands echo throughout the boat as the servants and crew begin tending to their appointed tasks.

Nefertiti gathers her precious brood to her like a mother hen.

"Now, remember children — Anie, Tut, Meri, Smenke — pay attention. You are all to stay close to me. We don't want or need another incident such as the one at the mastaba; besides, there is always the possibility that a fanatic might want to harm us. Security should be tighter here at Giza."

Anie approaches her mother with a quizzical look. "Mother, do you always have to call us children?" She pauses a moment. "After all, we really aren't children anymore — at least I don't feel like a child;

in fact, I am having some very womanly feelings."

At first Nefertiti is taken back a little with surprise but as she stands looking at this lovely creature, she realizes that the face and eyes and body are maturing and indeed a beautiful young woman is emerging. Yes, she tells herself, Anie is much older in appearance and in manner than her age would suggest.

Smenke interrupts the serious discussion with his boyish enthusiasm.

"The gangplank is down! Let's go!"

A feeling of anticipation fills the air as the caravan is hurriedly assembled. After everything is in order they are ready for the journey to Giza where the great pyramids and the Sphinx await their visit. It will not only be reason to see the wonderful monuments, but to celebrate their religious significance.

Upon arrival at Giza, they observe a village crowded with people and animals. Wooden wheeled carts are slowly making their way up and down dusty streets, pulled by stubborn flea-bitten donkeys. The poor beasts bray their resentment as their backs are beaten upon unmercifully by aggressive masters yelling their wares for sale. Their sharp cries pierce the foul-smelling air.

Peasant women are busy with their push-carts trying to barter home-grown fruits and vegetables. Some carts are layered high with brightly covered pieces of fine linen that the women have woven themselves, all for sale to the highest bidder. Others have clay jugs filled with precious oils — castor oil, flaxseed oil and sesame oil — highly prized and essential products needed by everyone. The oils are used not only for cooking and for burning in their lamps, but for religious purposes and for cosmetic uses.

Curious onlookers pay their respect to the royal entourage as it gropes its way through the smelly and crowded streets. Some begin following in single file. There is a stark contrast between rich and poor.

The caravan, now with many villagers who have joined the pilgrimage, makes its way through the main street until it comes to the end of the town. Then continuing for a short distance, it comes to a halt.

"There they are!" It is Smenke again yelling loudly.

And there, sitting majestically on the sandy hills of the Giza Plateau are the three great pyramids with the awe-inspiring Sphinx lying silently in front as if to guard the secrets of eternity.

"Let's get closer!" Smenke is bursting with excitement as he stands next to Tut. He and Tut have studied diligently about these extraordinary objects.

Tut is just as excited as Smenke but, in his usual subdued manner, does not express his feelings quite so openly.

Anie and Meri are more interested in their own personal happenings and are busy chattering away with each other in their girlish manner.

The first stop is in front of the great Sphinx. It has acquired the name of Hor-em-akhet, meaning Horus-in-the-horizon. This is in reference both to Horus the god and the akhet sign. The akhet is rendered as a sun between two mountains. Viewed from the Sphinx at the time of the summer solstice when the sun is at its greater distance north of the celestial equator, it sets directly between the pyramids of Khufu and Khafre. Anyone approaching from Memphis can see the head of the Sphinx silhouetted between the two pyramids.

Since this is a religious pilgrimage, the villagers have painted the head of the Sphinx red and graced it with ornaments.

As Nefertiti stands in her assigned place for the ceremonies, noting the serenity and mystery of the Sphinx's massive face, Anwar steps forward and begins speaking. All stand engrossed. Even Anie and Meri begin to listen:

"Built a little over thirteen hundred years ago, the question is, why did the Pharaoh Khafre want the Sphinx and its temple in the first place? These two features are totally new. It was traditional for a pharaoh to have a pyramid, a mortuary temple adjacent to it, and a 'valley temple' on a lower level for various purification rites.

"We have concluded that it was a solar temple — the oldest known in Egypt. There are niche-sanctuaries on its east and west sides dedicated to the rising and setting sun, a colonnaded court with twenty-four massive pillars marking the twenty-four hours of the day, and twelve statues of the pharaoh. It is suggested that the Sphinx was not placed to guard the Giza necropolis as some have surmised, but instead was a symbol of the sun-god himself, peering over the colonnade into the sanctuaries below.

"It is further believed that the Sphinx represented the Pharaoh Khafre as Horus, the god of Kingship, presenting offerings to the sun-god in the solar temple. If correct, then the Sphinx and temple complex may well represent the crucial transition, known to have taken place about the time of Khufu and Khafre, toward a solar-oriented religion. Before that time Horus, represented as a hawk, had been all powerful, but with the rise of the solar cult he had to make way for the sun-god Ra.

"The Sphinx was cut from the top down into the limestone bedrock. A prodigious amount of stone had to be hacked away all around it."

"Its sheer size is awe-inspiring. It measures seventy feet from the top of its head to the base of the monument. Its lion-shaped body is 150 feet long with paws fifty feet long. A sunken temple lies beneath its paws."

"Since the Sphinx has come to represent the sun-god, and since this is the center for the special cult, we are happy to be here today for this religious pilgrimage."

Nefertiti nods approval to Anwar for his very informative remarks, and asks him to continue.

"Also, although there is a lot of sand around it now, you can still see the outline of the long causeway from the Sphinx to the Funerary Temple. Boat pits are located on each side. The causeway — limestone pavement and passage beneath it — enabled people to reach the other side without walking around the pyramid complex. Its walls are adorned with reliefs and sculptures that show the same workmanship as the pyramid itself."

But it is the appearance of the pyramids that fascinate Smenke, Tut and Anwar even more. They stand mesmerized, gazing and drinking in the luxury of such a wonderful experience. They know that this opportunity is not granted to all.

The braying of donkeys in the distance catches their attention as they observe priests and a sizable representation of the local citizenry approaching the Sphinx for the morning rituals. Dust from the procession creates an almost mystic illusion.

Searing heat of the day, reflecting off the hot sand, gives a mirage effect, making it difficult to distinguish reality from the mysterious.

Upon arriving at the Great Sphinx the priests perform their ritualistic duties, praising the sun-god Ra and paying homage to his presence as evidenced by this magnificent creation.

Village priests end their devotions and ceremony. The peasants disperse and slowly make their way back to their homes and businesses.

Anie and Meri stay with Nefertiti and enjoy liquid refreshment under the shade of a tent.

As Tut, Smenke and Anwar stroll around the bases of the pyramids, Anwar speaks and points to the largest pyramid:

"Pharaoh Khufu built this pyramid over thirteen hundred and fifty years ago. It is the mightiest of all. By this time it had become traditional for an Egyptian pharaoh, early in his reign, to start building a pyramid for his memorial and final resting place."

Anwar continues: "Pharaoh Khufu's son, Khafre, succeeded his father as pharaoh and started building the second pyramid about forty years later.

"Pharaoh Menkaure, was the son of Khafre and grandson of Khufu. He started construction of the third pyramid about thirty years later."

Tut stares upwards at the immense monuments. Blotting out the busy activities taking place about him, he tries to picture in his mind how this area had looked before the tons of sand covered and buried its secrets. He wonders how this all came to be. His thoughts turn to a theory he and Smenke studied earlier.

"Let's all go out on that plateau and re-enact how the mighty pyramid was first begun," he suggests.

"That's a fine idea," agrees Anwar.

"Let's go!" shouts Smenke.

The three run hastily over the sandy hills to an area that is fairly level.

"Here are some sticks that I have brought along," says Anwar as he pulls the items from under his robe. He is prepared for all kinds of situations and looks like a magician pulling tricks from his sleeves. Being the good teacher that he is, he seems to possess that special quality of perception.

"Tut, pace off several steps and drive this stick into the ground." "Smenke, you take this piece of papyrus twine and loop it around the stick, and bring the loose end back to me." Smenke does as he is told.

Anwar ties the loose end around a longer stick and hands it back to Smenke. "Now, Smenke, keeping the string tight, drag the stick through the sand and walk around the stick that Tut has driven into the ground. This will give us a perfect circle."

"Now we shall pretend that this circle is a low stone wall with a top that is perfectly horizontal. Tut, you stay by the stick in the center. Smenke, you go stand inside our imaginary wall." Tut stands by the stick in the center as directed, and Smenke stands near the 'wall.'

Anwar continues: "I am imagining that a certain prominent star in the northern heavens is visible. Smenke, pretend that all of a sudden you see the rising star."

"I see it right now," yells Smenke, happy to cooperate with his tutor.

"You are to alert Tut immediately."

"Tut, there it is!"

As Tut stands next to the stick, he replies, "I am taking a bearing on the star. Mark its position on the wall, Smenke."

"It is marked."

"That's fine." Anwar is pleased that the boys are enjoying this important lesson.

"As you know, the procedure we are doing must be repeated a second time twelve hours later when the star arches across the sky. And to check the accuracy of this procedure, it must be done again several more times."

"Now Smenke, pull the twine toward the two points on the ground immediately below the marks on the wall. By cutting in half the angle thus formed, we have a line running due north and south — the other two points are at right angles to it. Now we know how and why the four sides of the pyramid are accurate." The four sides of the pyramid are aligned almost exactly on true north, south, east and west.

Anwar motions to the boys. "We had better get back to the others." His lean tall figure moves towards them. Being seven and one-half years their senior he possesses qualities that are those of a mature male.

Anwar is becoming a little apprehensive. There never seems to be enough guards to protect the royal family and, as he looks about, he cannot see any nearby.

All of Anwar's thoughts aren't filled with the safety of Tut and Smenke. There is another reason for his desire for a quick return to the others. The first time he had seen Ankhesenamun he couldn't keep his eyes off of her. Of course, he assures himself, that many others feel the same way. After all, her beauty is something that stands out. Besides, he is just a tutor and not of royal blood. And yet, when her heavy dark lashes sweep upward, revealing eyes of beauty and innocence staring into his, he feels an uncontrollable desire to hold her close. "That is just a feeling of protectiveness," he keeps reminding himself again and again. He wishes he could convince himself of that.

Anwar and Tut agree that it is time to join the others. It is Tut who seems to possess an instinct of awareness also — very different from the happy-go-lucky Smenke. With Smenke they return to the base of Khufu's pyramid where the others of their group have assembled. Everyone is sharing their enjoyable experiences. They coax Anwar to continue telling them more about the history of these pyramids.

Anwar voices more interesting facts. "After completion of determining and marking the site for the pyramid, thousands of men were delegated to work on the gigantic building program. Masons, carpenters, bricklayers, quarriers, painters and laborers were needed — men from villages all along the Nile. Also, hoards of peasants who could leave their farms during the inundation season were needed. The men volunteered their services because of their loyalty to and love of the Pharaoh, and were grateful for favors given to them by their local gods. Slaves were used to help care for the workers by cooking, cleaning and doing their laundry."

"These gangs of men — a total of 100,000 or more — worked in groups of about twenty on each assigned project for three months. About 4,000 were regularly employed at a time throughout the year. At the end of their three months, another group took over. They had to live at the building site, so quarters were constructed over there." Anwar points to the rubble nearby.

"There is evidence of this existing now. Just think, there were many streets with tiny stone row-houses. The quarters were small but adequate. I am sure the larger rooms were used for serving food."

"Later, when the pyramid was completed, mastaba tombs were needed for the deceased high priests, nobles, officers of state and for those of the royal household. All wanted to be near their dead Pharaoh in his afterlife and to serve him as they did while on earth. You can still see remnants of some of these near the base of the Pyramid."

"The pyramid is joined to the riverbank by a mile-long causeway. At the foot of the causeway, near the Nile's edge, is a building where embalmment rituals were performed. Near the pyramid itself is a mortuary temple. At the time of the completion of the pyramid, the causeway was roofed and had a long enclosed corridor, its walls covered with sculptured relief. Some of this is now buried beneath the sand."

"Attached to the pyramid is a chapel, reached by a long stone causeway which runs from the plateau down to the temple. Here stands an immense, magnificent statue carved in the likeness of the dead Pharaoh. Near one of these causeways, and connected to it, is the great Sphinx." Anwar points to it.

"Now it's my turn," tunes in Smenke. "After the first three important phases were taken care of — namely the selection of the site, recruitment of the men, building of the barracks and road — naturally the foundation of the pyramid was of utmost importance as it had to sit on absolutely level ground."

"I wish we could do the water level experiment like we did the site measuring one, but we don't have time to dig the trenches. I think I can explain from what you have taught me how the ground under the pyramid was leveled." His young voice keeps a constant chatter with a note of keen interest.

"Trenches were dug about the base of the site and then filled with water. Clay jugs were used to carry water from the river for this purpose. At one of these filled trenches a man held a piece of papyrus twine tied to a stick. A second man, on the other side of the connecting trench, held the other end of the taut twine, also tied to a stick of equal length and held touching the water. Several perfectly straight sticks were placed in the dry ground between the trenches; the ground was then leveled until these straight sticks showed the floor was parallel to the twine."

"Good for you, Smenke," says Anwar. "Did you know that there are underground burial chambers beneath the pyramid?"

"No," Smenke and Tut reply in unison.

"It's true, and they still exist today in an unfinished state. Apparently Pharaoh Khufu changed his mind and had his architect plan these chambers in the heart of the pyramid. A new ascending corridor, called the 'Grand Gallery,' was driven upward through the masonry at a steep angle."

"May we see it?" Tut asks anxiously.

"Yes, but now it's time for all of those who want to enter the pyramid with me to form a line," replies Anwar, waving a signal with his right hand. Tut and Smenke rush to be first in line.

"I must warn you of the steep climb and little air in the Grand Gallery."

The line shortens as Anie, Meri and their servants head toward large stone blocks in a shady spot nestled against the pyramid. "We will wait here," they echo.

It is Nefertiti who cannot be persuaded to forego the experience of entering the pyramid. She takes her place in front of Tut. "I want to see the inside," she persists.

Single-file, the group walks slowly through the entrance. Oil lamps hanging on the roughened walls create strange, shadowy images like dancing ghosts. Only the voice of Anwar breaks the eerie silence: "There is a horizontal passage to our right that descends into a small chamber. This was built supposedly for the burial location. A niche was even made in the wall to hold a statue of the pharaoh. Due to a change in plans — probably for security reasons — Khufu had a new chamber built at the top of the Grand Gallery to which we will now ascend.

Inside temperatures are rising steadily and there doesn't seem to be much circulation of air. Hands are placed in the carved-out recesses along the walls to assist in the steep climb. Stone steps have been chiseled out of the hard rock with strips of wood nailed into each one to provide better support for the feet. It would be a long fall from the slippery stone.

The stretched rope along the way also helps to pull their hot bodies upward. And hot they are!

Sweat runs profusely down their faces. Wet clothing clings to their bodies. Grunting and panting are the only audible sounds. Body odors are unpleasant.

Suddenly, a voice rings out: "Catch her!" "She's falling!" Nefertiti's limp body falls backward into Tut's outstretched arms.

"Are you all right?" a worried Tut asks, "Answer me, please." His pleas are in vain.

"Get her down and outside immediately, orders Anwar. He suspects that she has fainted. Gently she is carried through the small opening and out into the fresh air.

"Get some water!" Tut places her in the shady area next to a worried Anie and Meri. "She is going to be fine," he assures them. A cool linen cloth is placed on the Queen's forehead.

"What happened," an awakening Nefertiti asks as she opens her eyes. I feel so foolish. I wanted so much to see more of the inside of the pyramid."

"Just take it easy." "We are going back into the pyramid." Tut waves to Anwar and Smenke and they walk back to the entrance of the pyramid.

In a way, Nefertiti is pleased that her fainting spell was due to the lack of air in the Grand Gallery rather than she being pregnant. Previously, when she was with child, fainting spells were common. She realizes that she is getting to the age when she no longer desires to have more babies. Her children are growing up and she is looking forward to being with and enjoying her grandchildren.

Inside the pyramid the small group ascends the steps again and approaches the top of the Grand Gallery. As Tut pulls himself up the steep incline he can't help noticing the unusual type of corbeled construction above him. It is a projection of timber from the face of a wall arranged lengthwise to support an overhanging weight — placed under a girder to increase its strength. He is aware that this is one of the finest surviving works of early Egyptian history.

He is now at the top of the Grand Gallery where there is an entrance that opens into the King's Chamber. "What a relief!" Tut groans as he lowers himself into the large, dark granite room that is in the very heart of the pyramid. Oil lamps dimly light the windowless room, and the smell of burning oil hangs heavy in the air. As he glances upward at the high ceiling he can only imagine the tremendous weight above him.

Tut notes that the masonry work is superb, but the room is not level and seems to tilt slightly at one corner.

Walking to the middle of the room, Tut notices an ugly, dark, lidless granite sarcophagus. It sits alone and empty. As his hand touches the hard surface, he wonders why a pharaoh who could build such a magnificent tomb for himself would settle for this dismal burial chamber.

Looking up, Tut sees small openings near the ceiling. Anwar explains that these are air vents leading to the outside. "We believe the Queen was buried directly below this room. The workmen who created that vent probably joked among themselves that the Queen could shout her instructions directly to her husband even in death."

Smenke notices another small opening in the wall. "Doesn't this one lead down to the other chamber below?"

"Yes," replies Anwar. "And, as we believe, the 'Ka' spirit can now make its way about the tomb, such as in the mastabas, where a false door is made for that reason."

As the small group stands together, a tremendous feeling of reverence envelopes them in an invisible shroud.

"We must be on our way." Anwar ushers the boys to the opening. "We want to walk over to the river's edge where the building stones were brought to build the pyramid." Going first through the opening he then helps guide them back down the treacherous stairway.

Fresh air fills their stifled lungs as they emerge into the bright sunlight. Tut and Smenke run to see Nefertiti. She assures them that she is fine.

Nefertiti announces that the visit must end soon. She gives a nod of command to guards nearby. They know that their assigned task is to keep an eye on the three who are now walking out into the desert.

Portions of a once much-trod roadway stretch vacant and silent out into the dry, hot, sandy hills. Anwar leads the way with Tut and Smenke lagging close behind.

The mile-long hike brings them to the site where they can see evidence of the same channel that had been so heavily used those many years ago. The giant limestone blocks were brought on sturdy barges from the Mokattam Hills, located on the opposite bank of the Nile, where the quarries were twenty-eight miles east of Giza. Also, the granite used for the burial chambers and the Great Gallery had been transported in similar fashion from Aswan in Upper Egypt.

"Those quarries were busy places, weren't they?" asks Smenke.

"Yes," replies Anwar. "Can you imagine that more than two million stone blocks were needed to build the pyramid — most of them weighing two and one-half tons each. The stoneworker first marked the levels of stone in the quarry before they were divided. To cut a block of limestone, a hardened copper saw was used. Sand was used as an abrasive to increase the cutting power. A piece of twine or even a wooden stick can cut granite when used with a sand abrasive.

"Also, the saws had jeweled cutting points probably of beryl, topaz, chrysoberryl, sapphire or hard uncrystallized corundum. These jewels were removed and set in pieces of fine jewelry later.

"Drills were formed by bending saw blades into a circle. They could cut a circular hole by rotation. If the cutting edge was held stationary, the work could revolve around it like our diorite bowls are made. They are too accurately cut to be made by hand."

Anwar continues: "Special dolerite hammers were used to chip rough gutters or slots in quarry walls. Workers then fitted wooden wedges into the slots; soaked with water, the wood expanded and split off chunks of rock. The massive stone chunks were then hammered into rough blocks. The stone was eased onto long rollers and slid smoothly to a ramp. At the end of the ramp, workmen loaded the block onto a wooden sledge. By using rollers, ramps and sledges work gangs were able to haul those blocks, weighing up to 15 tons each, from quarry to barges along the Nile, hundreds of yards away."

Tut interrupts: "That was something!" "And without draft animals or even the wheel." "And to drag and haul all of them first from the quarries to the river, float them across to here on barges, and then drag and haul them again to the building site was a monumental feat!"

"Monumental, indeed," replies Anwar.

With several royal guards still standing nearby, the three start their short journey back to the pyramid.

"I think I know how the stones were probably used to build the pyramid," says Smenke.

"Tell us," urges Anwar.

"After the stones for the base were layed, a ramp of earth and rocks was built up to it. Then the stones for the next level were dragged up. When that level was laid, the earth ramp was raised again, ready for the next level to be built. As the ramp rose continually on all four sides of the pyramid, the angles of the slopes remained the same. For efficiency, there were three ramps running up and one going down. Heavy blocks were maneuvered into place by strong wooden levers." When the last stone was in place at the top of the pyramid, the earthen ramps were removed revealing the completed pyramid."

"And remember," adds Anwar, "The joints were cemented throughout. Even though the stones were brought as close together as 1/5000th of an inch — or into contact — the mean opening of the joint was 1/50th of an inch, those skilled builders still managed to fill the joint with cement in spite of the immense size and weight of the stones."

"And when the pyramid was completed Anwar continues: it is told that it was covered from top to bottom with a smooth polished casing of fine limestone. Then the top was capped by an apex of granite so brightly finished that the first rays of the sun bounced off of it like living fire."

A smiling Anie and Meri greet them on their return. They are all anxious to board the royal yacht for the long journey home to Tell El Amarna.

The light of day is gradually giving in to the inevitable darkness.

Safely back on the luxurious yacht, with the north winds blowing triumphantly against its raised sails and pushing it up the river, two figures stand at the bow — Tut and Anie.

Tut places his arm around Anie as she stands cuddled to his side. Looking down into her beautiful eyes, he whispers softly: "When I am Pharaoh of Egypt, you will be my Queen."

"Maybe I shall build a great pyramid just for you."

"A STAIRCASE TO HEAVEN IS LAID FOR HIM SO THAT HE MAY CLIMB TO HEAVEN THEREBY."

(Pyramid Texts)

WAR AND INCEST

The terrible wars are continuing in Syria, Palestine, Libya and the Sudan. Egypt is feeling the effects of the resource-draining defensive struggles.

Continually refilling the royal coffers because of the constant withdrawals of revenues is becoming a major problem. Gold mines are working day and night to produce the precious ore needed to finance the wars.

Families are distraught at seeing their male population maimed and, worse yet, some never returning home again. Battlefields are strewn with human bodies, swollen and decaying in the hot sun. Some become banquets for eager bands of snarling black jackals that slink about. They wait like actors in the wings to appear on their appointed cue and then devour the spoils of war.

Religious upheaval continues at an alarming rate. The people are not happy with the order issued by their Pharaoh, Akhenaton, to have the name of Amun erased from every monument on which it appears. Only he and a few of his followers believe in the new religion and it seems unlikely that there will be complete changes made.

Because of the fight for Akhenaton's religious dominance and the unpopular foreign wars, Egypt is in much turmoil at this time.

Akhenaton's reception hall in the great palace at Tell El Amarna is filled to overflowing with numerous nobles, priests of every rank, government officials and guests.

Nefertiti's elegantly clothed body sits straight and calm in her position to the right of Akhenaton. Her headpiece of intricately detailed gold work reflects little sparks of sunlight like twinkling stars. One cannot help but detect the same starlike glimmer in her bright eyes.

Even the Pharaoh, with his small, strange body curled leisurely on his great gold throne, looks majestic with his outstanding headpiece. The gold vulture and cobra protrudes from his forehead and the gold false beard hangs securely in place under his chin.

Next to the Pharaoh's throne to the left and one step below, stands the High Priest Ay, dressed in his opulent robe. He is also wearing a high headpiece set with hundreds of tiny precious stones. It is beautiful to behold. The maze of color and workmanship created by the Egyptian craftsmen is unrivaled.

There are other reception halls but this one is of a beauty almost beyond belief. Large copper shields are hung all about on the high walls doing their duty by reflecting the sun's rays in appointed directions. The plastered walls are painted brightly in an assortment of colors in scenes of religious and daily life happenings. In one area a group of sculptors are busy chiseling out figures of the royal family from other hard stone walls. Immense stone pillars and the high ceiling are areas where hieroglyphs are carved to tell stories.

The low rumble of voices is broken as Akhenaton arises. There is a dead silence. With his right hand outstretched and holding the royal scepter, he lifts his head slowly. In a high tone his voice shrieks out over the large hall:

"We are winning, winning, I say — all of the foreign wars — all of them-we are winning!" he pauses and looks straight ahead.

"Egypt is triumphant in the fields of battle!" "Our chariot troops are the best, and the infantry is superb." "Our waterways have superior war ships with their ramming devices and manned with skilled oarsmen and pilots." He waves the scepter like a magic wand. A regimented line of black slaves march in carrying large baskets in their muscular arms.

"I have a surprise for all of you." "The contents of these baskets tell of our great victories!"

As the slaves kneel down, they lift the covers off the tops of the baskets. A groan of astonishment sweeps throughout the great hall.

"Count! — count and you shall see!" Akhenaton is reveling in his glorious show. The baskets are filled with human hands — hands that have been chopped off the arms of dead enemy soldiers. Only right hands are present. An accurate count can be made of the battle spoils.

He then turns to Ay: "And what do you have to report, High Priest?"

Ay is shocked. Can he really be seeing and hearing all of this? It is true that Egypt has triumphed in the foreign wars, but most of what has been accomplished has been over and done with for many years. The warships are indeed great ones, but they have seen their day of victories and the waters are now still. Few battles remain for them.

Before Ay can answer, the Pharaoh continues: "The power of Aton is over all of us!" "The new religion has taken hold and is now entrenched in both Upper and Lower Egypt."

The hush of the crowd now changes slowly to a roar as they seem to be coming to their senses. A burst of angry voices shout:

"That's not true! You are lying!"

"I am the Pharaoh! Believe in me!"

"No! No! It can't be!" the crowd yells in unison.

Nefertiti is aghast. She looks at Ay.

"Akhenaton has gone too far this time," he whispers in her ear. "I have tried to warn him but he pays no attention — it is to no avail. He and his fanatical beliefs are unpopular and he will have to suffer the consequences. Now he is adding lies to his mad-man beliefs."

The great hall is emptied quickly as the guards rush in and gently push everyone through the giant double doors before a full-blown riot can start.

Unobtrusively, Nefertiti rises and quietly leaves for her private quarters.

Ay tries to talk to Akhenaton. "The people are not ready or willing for any changes now. Can't you see that?" There is no answer.

"Bring my daughter, Ankhesenamun, to me at once," orders the Pharaoh brushing past Ay as if he is not present. He makes his way toward his own private quarters.

"Yes, your Highness," replies an obedient servant.

Ay can't believe what he is hearing. He must find Nefertiti at once. Maybe she has gone to Anie's room and he can warn them of the impending danger. Ay rushes to the corridor where his granddaughter's suite of rooms are, but no one is there. He then runs out into the garden hoping he will find them strolling along one of the pathways. They are nowhere in sight. Nefertiti must be in her own quarters, he thinks, so he hurriedly goes back into the palace and down the long hallway leading to her door.

Ay knocks gently: "If you are in there, I need to talk to you my daughter."

The Queen's maid servant opens the door a crack. "She does not wish to be disturbed." She hesitates. "Oh, I am sorry, your Excellency, I didn't know it was you."

"That is all right. Please tell her it is her father who wishes to see her at once."

"One moment, please." There is a hushed sound. "You may enter now."

"Thank you. You may leave."

Nefertiti is sitting quietly in her favorite pillowed chair as Ay makes his way to her side.

"I do not want to tell you this," he says hesitantly, "But I am afraid you might be right about Akhenaton and Anie."

She rises slowly and steadily from her chair. "Tell me what, father? If you know something that I don't, you must tell me at once."

"A little while ago—after you had left — Akhenaton ordered Anie to his quarters."

"Ordered?"

"Yes, I'm afraid so," he replies sadly.

Like a cat springing for its prey Nefertiti jumps from her chair and rushes out of the room, running as fast as she can down the long hallway. Turning at the end she hurries down a second hallway that leads to Akhenaton's private quarters. Her sandaled feet can't go fast enough for her. Ay and some of the servants have a difficult time keeping up with her. As she approaches the large, closed forbidden doors she can hear screams coming from within.

"No, no, don't — you are hurting me!"

Nefertiti can feel her heart beating faster, and faster as her chest tightens. She starts pounding on the door. "Leave her alone! Leave her alone!"

"Help, please help me — somebody!" There is a pause. "Mother, is that you?"

The pleas of anguish tear at Nefertiti's whole being. "You monster, let her go!"

Just then, Ay and the servants appear. "Break down the door," he orders.

The servants push their strong bodies against the stubborn wood and the doors fly open.

Akhenaton is rising from the disheveled bed. Ankhesenamun is curled fetus-like under the covers, sobbing uncontrollably. Nefertiti rushes to her daughter's side and cradles her lovingly in her arms. "Hush, hush, mother will take care of you."

Ay rushes at Akhenaton, knocking him to the floor. "You despicable man!" shouts Ay. "How could you do such a thing to your daughter — it's disgusting!"

"I am the Pharaoh — the Pharaoh of all Egypt." His eyes have a crazed expression.

"I don't care who you are, you have no right to sexually molest your own daughter," screams Nefertiti.

"Out, out — everybody get out of here!" Akhenaton is yelling and moving about like a trapped animal. The commotion has drawn more spectators to the doorway. Nefertiti waves her maid servants into the room to assist her with Anie. They place a robe over the naked, quivering body and gently lift her into the wide corridor.

Nefertiti turns to Ay and says: "I am leaving the palace and I am taking Anie with me."

"Good," replies Ay, trying to comfort the tearful Queen. "Things will be taken care of here."

His eyes show a look that Nefertiti has never seen before — a very strange and dangerous look.

In the Queen's quarters Nefertiti holds a trembling and frightened young woman.

"I don't understand, mother, why would he want to do such a thing to me?" Then with a quick look of hurt in her face she looks up into her mother's face: "Oh, don't tell Tut, please — I wanted to be pure for him."

The small, pleading pathetic voice is almost more than Nefertiti can bear. "We are going away, you and I, to Maruaten, the summer palace. We will not stay here any more. I have already given instructions for the packing to begin."

It is a defiant, but hurt, Nefertiti.

7

TASHERY

"It is lovely here at the summer palace. I am glad you brought Ankhesenamun with you." "Are you sure you don't want me to bring Tutankhamun also?"

The Queen mother Tiyi is moving about in the beautiful sun room just off the dining area of the luxurious home. She is carrying a golden flask in her heavily jeweled right hand and every so often sips some of the white wine through her red-painted lips. Her loose gown covers a thick waist and full hips, but not the full breasts that protrude from underneath like two large melons. Chubby cheeks and puffy eyelids hide what once was a pretty face. She never was the beauty that her daughter-in-law is; however, there aren't many who can match the outstanding loveliness of Nefertiti except her own daughter, Ankhesenamun. Everyone agrees on that issue. Tiyi is a very pleasant and understanding, elderly woman.

Nefertiti is standing and gazing out over the large stone balcony. "Yes, Mother Tiyi, I think bringing Tut here is a good idea." "Meri and Smenke are coming for a visit soon, and I have also invited Anwar, as the tutoring should not cease."

Her eyes begin to cloud with tears. "And there is something you must know, but you must promise to keep it a secret — swear it to the gods."

"Of course I will." "What is it?" She surmises that is has something to do with her son Akhenaton. Rumors have already spread like wild fire concerning his state of mind. She is saddened deeply, but there is nothing she can do — he will not listen to her either.

"Anie is pregnant."

"The poor child," moans Tiyi. She doesn't have to be told the details; in fact, it clears any questions as to why Nefertiti is here. Her daughter-in-law wouldn't have left her son without good cause.

"For her sake, the secret will be well kept. Only Tahlia and a few other loyal servants who will be needed will know about it."

Nefertiti paces back and forth. "Above all, I don't want the other children to know about it. Anie won't show her condition for a few months so I don't think it will be a problem. And there is one other person we must take into our confidence — it is Anwar."

"Why the tutor?"

"I can trust him, and because I will need him later to help conceal the baby when it is born. I have thought this all out very carefully and there is just no other way."

The two women stand silently looking out over the lush valley. It has been a difficult time for both of them, but they know it is even worse for Anie.

Anie had gone to her mother shortly after the move to the summer palace and informed her of the ceasing of her monthly menstrual cycle. In turn, her mother had explained to her what had happened — most of which she already knew — that she is now pregnant following the rape by her father. In about nine months she will give birth.

Shock from the terrible experience engulfs Anie. Sitting alone for long periods of time she stares into space not wanting to talk to anyone. Tahlia tries to help comfort her. But, like many unhappy events in life, time becomes the only friend. After a while, Anie begins to adjust. Like a butterfly emerging from its cocoon, she feels much the same — emerging from her "child" cocoon and slowly becoming an adult woman. Sometimes she thinks that to just fly away would solve her problem, but she knows better.

Long visits with her Grandmother Tiyi, and the love she extends to her, help immensely. Also, news that Tut, Meri and Smenke are coming for a visit, lifts her spirits.

But now it is time for Tiyi to leave as she feels she must return to her residence in Memphis. It is her home and she doesn't care to be away too long. It is a long distance from Thebes (about 200 miles). Tell El Amarna is about half way, so she plans to stop there and visit her son. As a mother, it is very difficult for her to accept the fact that Akhenaton is acting the way he is, but she knows deep in her heart that he is a sick man. Even the Pharaoh of Egypt is human, she tells herself.

Tiyi waves a fond farewell to her loved ones.

Difficult times do not improve for Nefertiti. Current news received of Akhenaton and his few loyal followers remains the same regarding the war effort and his religious beliefs. She knows that the people will never accept the Aton cult and neither can she. She prays continually to her own gods to help relieve the inner hurt he has caused, not only to her but to one of his own daughters. Still possessing great powers of authority at the palace at Tell El Amarna, Nefertiti orders extra guards assigned to protect Meritaten and Smenkhkare. She knows that Ay will keep good surveillance in her absence, but she also knows that the priests are divided in their loyalty to the King. The best she can hope for is that Ay's group is more persuasive and more in number.

The mercy of time once again helps as the months pass quickly. Meri and Smenke are brought for a long visit and there is happiness and laughter throughout the rooms of the summer palace. Grandmother Tiyi brings Tut and then leaves after a few days to return to her home in Memphis.

There is a great change in Anie with Tut's presence. It is like a breath of spring for her as her downheartedness is uplifted. Smenke and Meri amuse her and all four socialize well together. They suspect nothing of Anie's condition.

One sweltering afternoon a figure appears at the entrance of the palace and is whisked quietly to Nefertiti's private quarters. It is Anwar. She is pleased to see him and she knows he is very capable of handling difficult situations. When informed of Ankhesenamun's condition, he is furious. He quells his outer emotions realizing that if he shows too much alarm he will not be included in the plans to help care for the princess, and later when the baby is born. He knows his feelings are beyond those of trusted servant and tutor. He has fallen in love with her. When he conducts classes for the royal group, he is aware that he must hide his secret well, and no one must suspect his true feelings.

As Ankhesenamun's mid-term pregnancy approaches, Tiyi arrives for a visit. While in the privacy of Nefertiti's sitting room she informs her that she thinks the stay of Meritaten, Smenkhkare and Tutankhamun — referring to them in their full names as she always likes to do — must come to an end. "It's going to become more difficult to make excuses about Ankhesenamun's physical condition. If the secret is to be kept, they must leave soon."

"Yes, you are right. She is beginning to gain more weight and they will begin to question this."

Looking directly into Tiyi's eyes she continues: "I believe an extended trip down to Aswan for Anie and me is the answer, and, of course, Anwar must accompany us." "You must return to your own residence, Mother Tiyi, and, as usual, Tut will stay with you for his own sake. He needs you even more now to supervise his upbringing, his education — and to protect him." She adds: "Meri and Smenke will return to Tell El Amarna."

As they are both agreeing that this is the best plan, a servant appears in the doorway telling them that a messenger has arrived from the Palace at Tell El Amarna.

"Send him in at once," orders Nefertiti.

The messenger is ushered in promptly and hands her a papyrus roll, tied and sealed with a royal emblem. She recognizes the seal as that of her father, the High Priest Ay. The messenger gives a polite bow and silently leaves the room.

"It's from Ay and he says for us not to worry that everything is being taken care of."

She hands the message to Tiyi and they look at each other a little bewildered. Such a brief message — and it really doesn't mean anything to them.

Tiyi rises. "I will go now and tell Ankesenamun

goodby and inform Tutankhamun that we are leaving."

Still bewildered, Tiyi reads the message again. "I really don't understand what Ay is trying to tell us." She shrugs her shoulders. "I'm sure he will explain in due time."

"Thank you so much for your love and understanding. I don't know what I would have done without you. I shall keep you informed." Nefertiti gives her a warm hug.

Tiyi waves a sad farewell. She knows it is going to be difficult to tell Tutankhamun that he won't be seeing Ankhesenamun for a while. But they have been separated many times before so she hopes it will not be too great of a problem. After they are gone, Nefertiti, in her usual organized manner, issues many orders for the trip down the Nile to Aswan. Elephantine Island will be the best place to stay, especially for safety and secrecy.

Anwar is a great help to her as he demonstrates his needed skills as a scribe at such a time by writing and contacting the numerous people who will be part of the scheme. Most will be informed that it is only another royal voyage and vacation time for their Queen and one of her daughters. Only a few of the most loyal and devoted are included in the true plan.

Meanwhile in Anie's room the servants are busy preparing for the long voyage.

"I hate to leave in a way, Tahlia, but in another way I know it is best for everybody. I'm glad mother decided that you will be with me as I shall need you very much when the time comes for the birth of the baby. I really don't know what to expect and I also don't know how I could do it without you."

"Don't worry, I have helped deliver a baby before,

so I will be prepared to do everything possible to help you."

After many days on the Nile the royal barge deposits its passengers on the banks of Elephantine Island. Needed supplies will be easily transported from across the river at Aswan. A large home of one of the wealthy nobles in the district has been volunteered for the royal family's use and, since the owner will be away for several months, the problem of secrecy and privacy is solved.

Guards are posted all around the small island.

It takes time for everybody to settle themselves in the new and smaller surroundings, but before they know it, the days pass into weeks and the final month of Anie's term is approaching. Her pregnancy has been uneventful and a healthy one with her small body, now round and full, carrying the precious living being within. Her beautiful face glows with an extra fullness and light that only motherhood can display.

Tahlia is her constant companion, always nearby when she needs her.

And when the days become too long for her to endure, there is always Anwar at her side to assist her in any way he can. His kind eyes and gentle voice always offer understanding. She tries to persuade herself that it is just that — understanding. But at times she notices a glint of affection. Of course, why not a little affection, she tells herself. She leans on him for his manly support and he is just doing his appointed duty as protector to a member of the royal family. In spite of what she is trying to convince herself, she knows she is beginning to more and more look forward to his presence. Their visits on the walks along the uneven shoreline become oftener and longer. She has to keep reminding herself that it is Tut whom she loves and hopes to marry some day.

Nefertiti keeps busy with the daily task of supervising the needs of everyone as the servants have to be instructed in their household tasks of cleaning, shopping, caring for the grounds, laundering, cooking, etc. She too enjoys the daily strolls along the river's edge and it is a relief for her to know that she can get away from her daily routine. She always worries, even though she knows that the house is being cared for with capable help.

It is one of those gloomy-looking days with gray skies blotting out the bright sun when Nefertiti joins Anie, Anwar and Tahlia for one of their leisurely strolls along the banks of the Nile. They are chattering happily when one of the servants comes strolling up to them with a messenger following closely behind, picking his way slowly over the uneven ground. It is a welcome sight as messengers have been rare. The trip to Elephantine Island from the palace at Tell El Amarna is a long and arduous undertaking.

The messenger had arrived on a large red barge that is awaiting his return. It is tied up at the dock. He had stopped at Aswan first as ordered by his superiors and was directed here after careful scrutiny by security guards. When they had seen the royal seal on the documents he carried they knew the Queen would allow his presence on the island. He carries two rolls of papyrus neatly tied and sealed. Leaning over in a polite bow he hands them to the Queen.

Nefertiti's fingers tremble as she unrolls the first one with the Pharaoh's seal visible. Detailed hieroglyphic writing is boldly evident. The signature of Akhenaton as Pharaoh of Egypt on the document is like a slap in the face, especially when she finishes reading it. Her skin turns pale as she hands it to Anie.

"As you can see, our marriage vows have been officially terminated. The Pharaoh has this authority, of course, and the high ranking priests must obey his wishes."

"Oh mother, I am so sorry!"

"Please, it's all right. I have been expecting this. It is no surprise, really. When I left him I knew that was the end of our marriage."

Anwar and Tahlia stand in silence.

"What message is in the other roll?" Anie asks curiously.

Nefertiti slowly unties the second roll and this time a look of astonishment flashes across her face. She reads aloud:

"By the authority invested in me, I now declare the official marriage of myself to my daughter, Ankhesenamun." There is an uneasy quietness in the room. "I further hereby order this information be chiseled into the walls of our great temple at Karnak for all to see." "I hereby sign and set my seal as Pharaoh of Upper and Lower Egypt.

"How can he do it? — wails Anie.

"I am appalled," replies her mother. "But the only bright note is that your child will not be a bastard. Your father does not know about your condition."

Anwar and Tahlia nod in agreement. Anie releases an uncomfortable sigh.

"Don't be upset about the news Your Highness," Tahlia consoles.

"It's not just that. I have a strange feeling, and it isn't the baby turning and kicking. It has stopped now."

"It is time," Tahlia states calmly. "I will take the princess to her quarters and help prepare her for the birth. I will need much help."

Arrangements are made by Nefertiti. Anwar volunteers to help but is hastily pushed aside.

"This is woman's work now," the Queen reminds him.

After being lead to her room Anie is undressed. A short gown is pulled down over her smooth shoulders and she is assisted carefully into her bed. The cool linen sheets, with the scent of fresh air still clinging to them, feel luxurious against her body.

Two hours pass and the beginning small pains that had spaced themselves several minutes apart are now beginning to become harder and closer together.

Tahlia orders more clean linen pads and a special small blanket to be in readiness. Warm water has been poured into a row of clay jugs.

"Tahlia, be sure to stay with me, won't you?" Anie clings to the strong black arms.

"Don't worry, my little princess, I am here. Take my hand and squeeze it hard when you need to." Now the long sharp pains are coming more frequent.

"Bear down — that's it — you are doing fine!" Tahlia instructs Anie the best she can with her limited knowledge. When the pains reach their excruciating point, Anie's sharp nails dig deeply into the outstretched soft palms of the loving servant.

"It's coming, it's coming — bear down once more — real hard! There's the head!"

And then, the miracle of life emerges into the world and all the pain ceases. Tahlia lifts the precious new-born baby carefully in her strong hands and announces to a worn out new mother: "You have a beautiful baby daughter."

As its sharp little cries ring out, they fill the room with happiness. Everyone heaves a sigh of relief. The other servants help Tahlia cut and tie the umbilical cord, remove mucus from its tiny mouth, bathe it in warm water and then wrap it gently in its proper blanket.

"I want to hold my baby." The new mother watches as Tahlia lifts the small bundle and brings it to her. She places it in the welcome cradle of its mother's arms. As Anie looks down at the pink face surrounded with a mop of baby-fine black hair, she is overwhelmed. Its eyes are tightly closed and the tiny fists are clenched like they are ready for a fight.

Anie's thoughts are jumbled. "She is so beautiful! Go bring mother at once so she can see her granddaughter." And then the proud mother proclaims: "Her name is Tashery."

All the time Anwar has stayed close to Nefertiti as he knows that she will be the first informed of the baby's birth. When the servant brings the news they are both overjoyed. Anwar is not allowed to see the baby yet, but the Queen rushes happily to see the new mother and her first grandchild. "Oh, she is so beautiful," she coos.

The days pass quickly as Ankhesenamun regains her strength and keeps busy nursing her baby. Tahlia is busy changing diapers and giving the infant its daily bath. And, of course, everybody wants to hold Tashery — including Anwar. He is allowed an occasional turn but is always reminded that he is not to spoil her. If she utters the slightest cry, there are many hands eager and ready to assist. It is Nefertiti who puts a limit on the holding of the baby. After all, it is her granddaughter and she has some say in the matter, so she thinks.

"I must leave you for a short period of time and go to Tell El Amarna. Abdul wants to see me."

Anie nods. "I know how much he means to you, Tahlia." "Are marriage plans in the wind for you and Abdul?" she teases.

There is no reply.

Anie sees a determination in Tahlia's face she has not seen before. Something important is afoot, but she does not wish to press the issue.

A few weeks after the birth of Tashery, a messenger arrives. This time the seal is not that of the Pharaoh but of the High Priest Ay.

As Nefertiti unties the papyrus roll, she enters a state of shock. The message reads: "Akhenaton is dead. Preparations are being made for his funeral. The mummification will be completed in the usual time of seventy days." The message ends with: "Smenkhkare has been proclaimed Pharaoh of Egypt."

It is not surprising that the Queen takes the news so hard. She had dearly loved her husband in the past, but she knows that deep in her heart she can never forgive him for what he did to their daughter. As her first thoughts clear, she begins thinking how strange that Ay has not given the reason for his death. But what perplexes her most is that Smenkhkare has been put on the throne.

Some time later, still another messenger appears. The message is from Ay again. It states that

Smenkhkare is dead. How strange that the deaths of Akhenaton and Smenkhkare are almost simultaneous. The rule of Smenkhkare is brief indeed.

Grief takes a tight hold of Nefertiti and Ankhesenamun. They both loved Smenke, remembering his happy-go-lucky and loving ways. And they think of poor Meritaten probably left with only her Grandfather Ay and Grandmother Tiyi to help console her.

After the first shock waves leave, Nefertiti knows that she must act quickly. Tutankhamun must be the next Pharaoh. And without Anie's knowledge, something will have to be done to provide a safe haven for Tashery. A hasty departure is necessary.

She sends for Anwar. "Now is the time that we planned previously. You must take Tashery away and have her raised in a safe place where nobody will know who she is. I shall help with the arrangements."

"Ankhesenamun will be broken-hearted," he states.

"Yes, I know, but it is the only way. For the sake of all and especially for the future of Egypt to continue as a great land, the banishment of Tashery is necessary."

"Your orders are obeyed."

A sad Anwar leaves quietly that night, helped only by two faithful and trustworthy female servants who will help care for the baby Tashery.

8

KARNAK

It is difficult to console Ankhesenamun after she has been informed of both her father's and brother's deaths. She feels guilty about her inability to forgive her father for his brutality toward her. But, Smenke's death grieves her greatly.

The disappearance of Tashery and Anwar are almost more than she can bear. At first she lashes out at her mother and then to Tahlia, who has returned from Tell El Amarna. They will not tell her where they have fled. She has to be reminded again and again that the secret must be kept. The longing to hold her baby close to her is not an easy matter to eliminate from her feelings. She keeps remembering the tiny body that had begun to grow and fill out from the nourishment she supplied from her full breasts, and how the skin was as soft as the petal of a flower. Wrapped in its blanket the little baby's body had felt warm in her cradled arm. She also misses Anwar's dark concerned eyes looking down at her as he caressed the baby's little arms and hands.

Nefertiti realizes it is time to leave Elephantine Island with Ankhesenamun and Tahlia. They leave with memories of great happiness and sorrow.

It is a long and sad trip up the river to Tell El Amarna.

Soon, everyone is settled back in their previous quarters where they have lived so long and have enjoyed so many good times. It is almost as if they had never left. But everything is changed now. An atmosphere of confusion and apprehension fills the air as Nefertiti barks orders like a nervous dog. Her first order is to see Ay.

The servants have no difficulty in locating Ay and informing him of the Queen's desire to see him. He is not surprised and there is much explaining to be done. He is ushered quickly into her private quarters. With a warm greeting and kiss, questions flow from her mouth: "What happened? How did Akhenaton and Smenke die? Where is Meri?"

Ay looks squarely into the troubled eyes of his daughter. Hesitantly he utters the words, "Naja haje."

Nefertiti takes a short step backwards in horror. "Oh no, I can't believe it!" "Not the cobra!"

"Yes," sighs Ay. "A hooded cobra somehow found its way into the Pharaoh's bedroom in the middle of the night. Akhenaton must have awakened and startled it. There were fang marks on his throat indicating where the poison entered his body. He must have had an agonizing death. He was not found until the next morning when the servants entered his room at their usual time."

"How terrible!" "And, Smenke?"

"Food poisoning."

This time the Queen stands stunned, and appears as if someone had waved a magic wand over her to ward off movement of any kind.

As she regains her composure, she asks: "How did it happen?"

"Meri and Smenke had eaten lunch together. Shortly thereafter, they had gone outside to play in the garden. Suddenly, Smenke became violently ill and collapsed on the ground. Meri thought he was playing a trick on her at first, but it was when he did not respond that she became frantic and began screaming and crying. Servants ran quickly to see what was the matter." Ay pauses. "It was thought that it must have been food poisoning even though Meri had not been affected by the food."

Nefertiti says, "Father, don't you think it unusual that both Akhenaton and Smenke, his successor, died within such a short period of time?"

Ay smiles knowingly and replies: "Those things happen sometimes."

"And what of Meri?"

Ay adds slowly: "Meri became uncontrollable."

With her senses fully regained by now, Nefertiti lowers herself into her favorite chair. "I wish to see Meri at once."

"I'm afraid that is impossible," replies Ay. "She has been sent away."

"Sent away!" "Where?" "Why?"

"She is in an institution in a small town up the river. There is little hope that she will ever be herself again. The shock of losing her father and then experiencing Smenke's horrible death was just too much for her."

"I shall make plans to visit her as soon as possible," a sad mother replies. "But now we must face the most important decision of the day and try not to dwell on these sad events. Egypt must have a ruler at once. I suppose Tut is still with Mother Tiyi at her palace in Memphis?"

"Yes, he is."

Nefertiti rises slowly and deliberately from her chair. In the gracious manner that she demonstrates so well she lifts her right arm and waves an order: "Bring him here at once!" "Tutankhamun will be the next Pharaoh of Egypt."

Ay nods in agreement. He knows she is right in declaring Tut as the new ruler. She has the power to declare who is next in line for the throne. Even though Akhenaton had declared termination of their marriage, and declared a marriage to his daughter, Ankhesenamun, Nefertiti's title as Queen of Egypt can not be taken from her. She retains her power.

As High Priest, Ay knows he has the authority to start the legal processes.

Ay asks: "And how is Anie?" "I appreciated your message about the birth of Tashery." As a small grin creases the folds around his mouth, he says, "I believe that makes me a great-grandfather." "I regret that I have not seen the baby, but I realize secrecy is important in this situation and I shall not disclose anything that has happened. The secret has been well kept. I destroyed your message, and Tut does not and will not know." He adds: "Our plans for Egypt and her future will always come first."

"Anie is terribly upset now but she is strong and I know she will be all right. It was severe action to take her baby from her but my plans —" Nefertiti hesitates and corrects herself, "— our plans — included that in our efforts." "She shall be Tut's bride after the coronation."

Again, Ay nods in agreement. "I must leave now. I have many things to take care of. The burial of Akhenaton and his ceremony are only weeks away.

As you know the mummies of both he and Smenke are being prepared."

After he leaves, Nefertiti decides to go to Anie's rooms where she knows she will find the broken-hearted loved one. Tahlia is there to greet her as she opens the heavy door.

"She doesn't want to eat anything," Tahlia whispers.

"Leave us, I want to talk to her."

Red puffy eyes show that Anie has been crying. Somehow she has heard about Meri and even how her father and brother died. As always, a network of information drifts throughout the palace walls like a chain reaction, mostly through the efforts of the servants. Rumors play their part, some of which hint that the two royal family members were murdered — by whom, no one will say.

"Don't cry, my dear, everything will be better soon, believe me."

Nefertiti holds her daughter close to her. "I have some good news for a change." Tut will be here soon." She knows this will awaken a new hope in her daughter.

The crying stops. "I can't wait to see him, mother. Do you think we can keep the secret of Tashery from him?"

"He will not know. And now for the important news — and it is especially for you — Tut will be the next Pharaoh of Egypt."

"I had not dwelled on the idea that he could be next in line for the throne. I guess in all of my own misery I had forgotten about that."

"Furthermore, after his coronation, you will be his Queen."

Anie is stunned for a moment. She knows that she always wanted to be his wife and, now after such a long time, it is about to happen — and to be his Queen also. "I can't wait to see him, especially now," she sighs.

Busy days follow for everyone in the great palace. Tut's arrival from his grandmother's residence seems to bring hope and a new feeling in the air. Kindness radiates from him naturally, touching all who come in contact with him. If he notices any difference in Anie he keeps it to himself because he loves her very much. The news that she is to be his bride has made him very happy. He too has been through some difficult days after losing his father and half-brother. He remembers the many good times he shared with Smenke. And even though he was never close to Akhenaton he is saddened by the way he died. He knows there was unhappiness between Nefertiti and the king, but he thought it was mostly their religious differences that had finally torn them apart. Any relationship between Anie and Akhenaton is the least of his thoughts.

Since Akhenaton had not been popular with the people at the time of his death, his funeral will be a small one. But as Pharaoh he is deserving of the very best according to tradition. His body is prepared properly for mummification, but not with the traditional Amun rituals. Professional grievers are hired as usual to follow the funeral procession and, on signal, will start their wailing and rubbing of dirt in their hair. And he will be buried in his prepared tomb on the west bank of Thebes in the Valley of the Kings.

On the east bank large mortuary temples have been erected and even larger ones on the west bank.

It was Akhenaton's father, Amenophis III, who was Pharaoh when prosperity reached its pinnacle in the busy city. At that time much of the vast wealth from foreign conquests poured into the temples of Amun.

Akhenaton reigned for seventeen years and for a brief time before his death Thebes fell on hard times because of the religious conflict. He had the name of Amun erased from every monument on which it appeared. The city was abandoned by the court because of the Amun cult. But his Aton cult and reform had not reached deep among the masses of population — if at all, as they preferred to keep all of their old religious customs and superstitions. Even the priesthood throughout the country fiercely opposed his work, but a few were silenced during his lifetime by force or bribery in some instances. There is always the handful who can be swayed, so there was a small group of priests who did accept the new ideas and remained loyal to their Pharaoh to the end.

As the High Priest Ay gives a brief eulogy for his son-in-law, tears do not flow from sorrowful eyes, neither his nor those present. Dutifully, the royal family accompanies the mummy of Akhenaton on the royal barge that crosses the Nile to his tomb along with his few faithful followers who are mostly priests. Ay reminds them that, even though the Pharaoh had been a religious fanatic, he had accomplished some great things during his life on earth. He had built a beautiful new palace and city at Akhetaton (Tell El Amarna). For the first time in history he had given his Queen, Nefertiti, equal prominence beside him, and had pictured the royal family as human beings rather than god-like idols to be worshiped from afar.

Ay does not mention the rift that had separated Nefertiti and Akhenaton; most knew nothing about it even though he had personally proclaimed the separation. Also, the marriage to his daughter, Ankhesenamun, is not mentioned.

Ay reminds his audience that although Akhenaton would let his imagination get carried away regarding the foreign wars' situations by making them sound better than they really were, there was some truth to his statements. There had been threats by Asiatic dominions, and from the east the Habiru did press into Canaan. In the north the Hittites had been a threat, especially with the Hittite King, Shubbuliliuma, spinning his web of intrigue with other petty kings of the Pharaoh's northerly provinces and inviting them to break away from Egypt.

Ay concludes the service with the words: "Akhenaton leaves his earthly existence to join his sun-worshiped god —'Bringer of Light and Life.'"

Shortly thereafter, Smenkhkare's funeral is held. This time the mummy is wrapped carefully and contains all the necessary jewelry, amulets and personal objects according to the Amun tradition. His grandfather, Ay, performs all the necessary religious rituals. Again, the royal barge crosses the Nile, transporting the small mummy in its carved wooden coffin. It is placed in a sarcophagus made of quartzite that has been awaiting its arrival in the special burial tomb. This time tears flow freely. He will be missed dearly by his loved ones. He has a right to a royal tomb, even though he officially was Pharaoh of Egypt for only a brief time. He is deserving of the high honor. Smenkhkare's strange death will never be understood.

Two Pharaohs have now been laid to rest, and another is being readied for the throne.

The coronation of Tutankhamun at Karnak is to be a great event. Not only the large city of Thebes will be taking part in the celebration but the small towns and villages along the Nile. All will join in the festivities that will last for many days. Preparations for parties and banquets are taking place all over the country — especially at the Palace at Tell El Amarna. Seamstresses are busy creating the detailed ornate gowns and robes that the royal family will be wearing. Artisans are painting and molding new works of art so outstanding that each piece will become a treasure. Cooks are listing menus to satisfy even the most finicky appetite. Scrubbing and cleaning crews abound throughout the palace. It is as if everybody and everything has come to life.

Tutankhamun is the center of attention. Nefertiti seems to be everywhere, making her way constantly in and out of the maze of rooms lining the long hallways. She is supervising every little detail with a sharp eye. The coronation must be perfect.

But it is the High Priest Ay who seems to be a more prominent figure by making his presence known with his gentle, but persuasive, orders.

Ay approaches his grandson's open doorway and strolls into the newly acquired quarters — those of a King. "We shall go to Karnak in the morning for a rehearsal. I believe Anie would like to accompany us and it is a good idea for her to see how the processional is handled since she will be marrying you soon after the coronation. She will be better acquainted with the temple layout."

"Yes, I want her to be with us."

"Good. I will go now and make the arrangements."

The next morning a large group of priests and servants accompany Ay, Tutankhamun and Ankhesenamun by boat to the small village of Karnak that lies near Thebes. This is where the site of the great temple is located. They are all standing in front of it... and great it is!

"Oh, Tut, it is massive in size and exudes a feeling of power — an obsessive type of power," says Anie. "I never realized just how awesome it is. You will have a long walk to the altar." She is in a teasing mood and enjoys being with her husband-to-be. Her soft hand slips onto his welcome arm and she gives him a touch of her warm presence as only lovers can do.

Ay steps forward proudly. "As you know, Akhenaton tried to abolish this place of worship in favor of his Aton religion and even went so far as to have the name of Amun erased from some of the walls, but it has been rededicated to our god, Amun-Ra, as it should be. It is the greatest and largest of all our temples and is really a complex of temples. The temple of the war-god Month is situated to the north; the goddess Mut — who we know is the wife of Amun — has her temple in the south. The greatest of all, of course, is this one in the center that we are about to enter."

"I want to know more about it. When was it first built?" Tut's eager interest prods Ay to continue.

"The exact date is unknown, but we do know that it was begun several hundred years ago as a small shrine to Pharaoh Senusret I. At the beginning of our time the Pharaoh Thutmose I approximately two hundred years ago, added the first great addition by enclosing it and fronting it with two central gateways, with a colonnaded room of cedar wood painted gold situated between."

Ay continues: "Queen Hatshepsut, about one hundred and twenty-five years ago, ordered completion of the works projected in the reigns of Thutmose I and II who ruled in succession just before her remarkable building reign. As depicted in reliefs on the walls of her incredible rock-cut temple at Deir el Bahri in the Valley of the Queens, she had two obelisks erected at Karnak that pierced the very temple roof."

"What a monumental project that must have been."

"Yes," replies Ay. "It was quite a feat as the two obelisks had to be transported by water from Aswan. They are ninety-five feet tall and weigh 700,000 pounds each. It took hundreds of men seven months to cut one. Then great levers were used to get the enormous stones onto sledges. The sledges were then hauled over rollers to the Nile's edge where an embankment of sand had been built over a large boat. Placed on the embankment, the obelisk was then lowered by removing the sand. The boat was then freed from the embankment and carried the obelisk up the river. Upon arrival at Karnak, a newly constructed brick ramp was used to haul the obelisk to its erection site. Once there, its base rested on a sand-filled hole over a block of stone. Gradually the sand was removed and the immense stone sank into the hole until it reached a vertical position. The sand was then removed and the obelisk stood in place."

"You will see these obelisks as soon as we go inside."

"Who built this pair of obelisks in front?"

"Following Queen Hatshepsut's reign, Thutmose III had those erected to celebrate the thirtieth year of his reign. They are over eighty feet high, six feet square at the base and weigh 143 tons each. He also added a jubilee pavilion and enlarged the temple. He is responsible for the wall that encircles the temple complex and had a sacred lake formed. Many of the additions to the temple were made in commemoration of victories in wars; others as offerings of thanks to the god Amun." Ay motions to look upwards.

"One of the carvings on the pylon shows Thutmose III grasping a group of bound captives in one hand and his other hand is holding a mace with which to bash out their brains."

"As soon as I become Pharaoh I shall add to the temple also," states Tut.

"I want to see where Tut is to be crowned — let's all go inside now." urges Anie.

Ay leads the way up an entrance ramp that opens into a forecourt. A gate is opened that admits them into an open court with covered colonnades on either side. At the far end of this inner court a ramp runs up to a columnar vestibule occupying the whole width of the building.

"This is where the ceremonies will take place," says Ay. "The temple area is really rather small compared to other areas, but it should be a beautiful service."

"The colors are so vivid," sighs Anie. "The red granite pillars seem to glow with beauty against the multi-colored paintings and inscriptions on the walls and ceiling. Queen Hatshepsut's obelisks are magnificent."

As Anie walks around them she can see that the Queen had her titles inscribed on each of the four sides. "She wanted to be remembered forever, didn't she?"

Anie looks up at the top of the obelisk. It is as if it has grown and gone through the roof and is on its way up to the sky. "The top is so beautiful with the shining electrum covering the obelisk. Rays from the sun reflect off of it appearing like little arrows darting about."

Anie hesitates and then remarks thoughtfully: "Our gods know we are sending our innermost thoughts and prayers to them through the sunbeam (tehen)."

She reads aloud the inscriptions: "...and you who after long years shall see these monuments, who shall speak of what I have done, you will say, 'we do not know how they have made a whole mountain of gold as if it were an ordinary task' ....to gild them I have given gold measured by the bushel, as though it were sacks of grain. And when my Majesty had said the amount, it was more than the whole of the Two Lands had ever seen.... When you shall hear this, do not say that is an idle boast, but 'How like her this was, worthy of her father Amun!"

Ay excuses himself from the group. As he walks through the hypostyle hall he too is thinking about how beautiful the building is.

Light and air enter through clerestory windows that are situated high above near the ceiling. They consist of huge granite slabs, pierced with two tiers of narrow, vertical openings. When the temple was being built, the columns in the central aisles were much higher than those at the sides to accommodate these windows. Cedar wood was used to support the roof and is painted gold. The richness of gold is everywhere. It covers ceilings, walls and doorways. Other colors of paint are used for decorations including greens, reds and yellows — all displaying a most beautiful effect.

From the colonnaded room Ay makes his way to the forbidden area where only he and a few of the other higher priests are allowed to enter — sometimes called the holy of holies. Here the shrine of Amun is hidden behind an enclosed wall with a small gate, and where the image of the divinity is kept in a sacred boat.

He walks down poorly lit corridors, lined with a series of small rooms, to reach the gate. The rooms are used for storing votive offerings and the like.

After he performs his accustomed religious duties, he joins the others back in the temple proper.

The rehearsal is brief as Ay explains the ceremonial route of the holy procession and where his grandson will be crowned as Pharaoh of Upper and Lower Egypt.

Anie re-enters the hall just when everyone is ready to leave. She dashes out a side entrance and enjoys viewing the lovely temple gardens and sees the splendid homes of officials lining the paths — high ranking priests and noblemen. Many officials of the state are fortunate to live in such a paradise. It takes many to operate a flourishing government such as this one.

"It's time to leave now," Tut calls to her.

"I am ready."

Making their way from the religious temple, silence and meditation floats about them like an invisible cloud. Anie stops at the entrance and, looking backward over her shoulder, she murmurs: "Its appearance of strength is almost terrifying."

She sighs, "Tomorrow will be a day to remember."

Tutankhamun's coronation at Karnak is spectacular. The years since his birth have been filled with special instructions to prepare him for this unique day. Nefertiti made sure of that. She has always looked upon him as her own son.

Tutankhamun goes through the long processional and hours of religious ceremonies in the great temple with an elegant performance. His grandfather Ay is always a step behind him making sure that all the procedures are carried out fully and to the extent of the law.

Finally, when the solid gold crown with the symbolic vulture and cobra protruding at the forehead is placed on his head, the handsome face of a young man beneath it shows a sign of relief. Now he is the Pharaoh of Upper and Lower Egypt. His loving eyes settle on only one — Ankhesenamun — his future Queen and wife.

It is difficult to tell who is the happier and prouder, Nefertiti or Ankhesenamun. They both beam with pride as they stand near his side. Both are dressed in gorgeous long flowing gowns embroidered in bright colors, adding still more elegance to the already majestic ceremony.

The celebration parties are to start in several days so everyone returns to their homes in Thebes. The royal family sails to their palace at Tell El Amarna. Festivities will take place all over the country — in every small town and village along the Nile. Weeks of preparation and planning have ended.

In her private quarters Anie has the company of Nefertiti who is busy instructing the servants with last minute details about seating arrangements for the party. It will begin in only a few more hours. She sends instructions to the chefs to make sure there is an abundance of food.

"You should lie down and nap for a while, my dear," Nefertiti urges in a motherly manner. "I know you will want to enjoy the festivities to the fullest this evening."

"I want to look my very best for Tut."

"By the way, mother, let's discuss Tashery and Anwar — and also Meri."

"It was to be a surprise, but I will tell you now. Anwar wants to attend your wedding in a few days, so he will be here at that time. He can give you news of Tashery then. And regarding poor Meri — it is a sad situation since there is little, if any, hope that she will ever be the same again. After your honeymoon, when Tut is busy with his new duties, you and I shall go to visit her." Then Nefertiti adds slowly: "And you will get to see Tashery."

That's all Anie needs to bring a look of brightness to her eyes — like seeing the flame in a just-lit lamp spring to life.

"Oh, mother, that's the most wonderful news. I shall have her in my arms again."

"But, I must repeat, you must remember that secrecy will be of the essence and Tut must not know. He will think we are only going to visit Meri."

"I understand. Don't worry. The secret is kept in my heart."

"I leave you now. See you at the party."

9

THE ROYAL WEDDING

Guests are beginning to enter the reception hall in the great Palace at Tell El Amarna. A small orchestra consisting of a lute, a double flute and a harp is playing softly in one of the alcoves. Drums and tambourines silently await their turn. Occasionally a trumpet blares to announce the appearance of a member of the royal family or an important official.

In one of the alcoves some guests are enjoying a popular game of Senet. They toss small sticks and move markers appropriately on the game board.

The hall has been decorated with fresh flowers placed everywhere. Some hang in garlands that are strung on pillars. Others are arranged in beautiful bouquets that bulge from huge vessels sitting at strategic locations for all to see. Lotus blossoms float in large shallow dishes. New wall hangings dangle brightly on the freshly-painted plastered walls. This all adds to the abundant colorful beauty.

Tables are piled high with all kinds of food. Very young serving girls, clad in nothing but necklaces, pour wine into solid gold goblets. Thirsty guests empty the goblets as fast as they are filled. Wine flows freely.

The lady guests, some of whom are seated in their own private alcoves, are separated from the men.

Each woman wears a fashionable, elaborate wig which falls to the shoulders in cascades of curls and braids. Sitting rigidly on top of the coiffure is a small cone of sweet-smelling pomade. With the heat from their body and from the warm temperature in the room, it slowly melts and oozes down the wig and over the shoulders — just enough to impart an oily, sweet-smelling odor.

They wear loosely-pleated robes of fine linen that reach to their ankles, girded around their hips with a pleated scarf which flares fan-wide at the end. Long, wide sleeves give each robe a distinctive appearance. One breast is left uncovered. Some wear a transparent, rippled shawl over their shoulders. Broad flower necklaces, bracelets and anklets complete their costumes.

The men wear a similar robe over an undershirt. Bracelets and the wide Egyptian semicircular breast collar complete their wardrobe.

Both men and women wear sandals of tooled leather or braided fiber. Some are encrusted with semiprecious jewels.

Ankhesenamun enters – a hush falls over the crowd. Tutankhamun has already arrived and taken his place on his newly-acquired throne. He watches her walk gracefully toward him. Everyone's eyes are on her. She is a vision of loveliness in her long, see-through green gown. The nipples of her breasts push against the gossamer sheer material. Her naked, slender young body beneath is covered only by a tiny undergarment. She moves about sensually. But it is her face, as always, that is so beautiful to behold. The green gown seems to turn her hazel-colored eyes a misty green, like the waters of the Mediterranean

Sea. Exotic outlining of black kohl, and the green malachite on her eyelids, make the eyes appear larger than normal.

Gliding across the tiled floor, she suddenly stops and acts as if she isn't sure which way to go. In front of her is Tut, but to the right is the designated place for the ladies to sit. As if reading her mind, Tut rises and descends the wide steps and walks across the long hall towards her. As he approaches, he takes her hand, turns, and leads her back with him.

"Bring a chair," he orders.

The crowd is surprised and delighted. Once again, Tutankhamun has shown human understanding and love. The people are more pleased than ever with their new Pharaoh.

Nefertiti, also looking outstandingly beautiful in a gown of white with gold threads woven throughout in an elaborate circular pattern, stands next to Ay. He looks majestic in his special ceremonial robe and crown. They exchange looks of pleasure.

"Let the celebration begin," shouts Tutankhamun.

The hall becomes a stage with the ever popular dwarf acrobats, jugglers, wrestlers and magic acts all performing in their proper sequence. Each event ends with great applause from a contented audience.

It is time for the finale. As the famous dancing girls appear, silence sweeps over the great hall. Wicks in the oil lamps are snuffed out with only a few left burning so as to cast a soft glow about the room.

The orchestra begins a slow, rhythmic, mystical beat with the drums and tambourines sounding in unison.

The row of scantily-clad young women slowly sway their bodies and approach the center of the room. Bare feet keep moving about in time with the haunting music. Their costume is only a long white skirt. Bare breasts bob up and down and glisten in the dim light.

But it is their hair that is outstanding. Each one has long, dark, thick hair that has been braided into a pair of pigtails. At the end of each long pigtail a heavy, round, metal disk hangs. As they dance, the metal disks are flung about in time with the music. It is an enchanting experience for all. They finish by lying outstretched on the floor. Their exit brings loud applause from the audience.

Then the feasting and drinking begins. And what a feast it is! These are the wealthy people of the land so food is prepared in abundance. They can always enjoy all sorts of vegetables and fruits — unlike the poor peasants whose diets consist mainly of bread, beans and salads made of onions or papyrus stalks.

At this banquet, tables overflow with selections of meat and fowl in addition to fruits and vegetables. For salads there are onions, lettuce and young papyrus stalks. Radishes, watermelons, cucumbers, peas and garlic are visible. Figs are piled high on a serving dish with grapes and dates circling them. There are nuts from the dom-palm. Roast meat from cattle of various breeds has been carved and stacked on large trays — from oxen, calves and gazelles. Another tray holds poultry with choices of roast geese and cranes, and succulent roast duck stuffed with bread. Fish from the Nile are arranged symmetrically on a platter. Small, conical-shaped loaves of bread sit alongside fried cakes sweetened with honey. Highly prized milk and milk products are readily available.

Wine continues to flow freely from the large pottery jugs. Each is labeled in ink with a docket stating vintage year and vineyard of origin.

Beer runs in close competition for consumption. Rich and poor alike drink beer. Their brewing technique produced a fine tasting beverage. They first bake coarse barley loaves, crumble them in a vat with water, stir and strain the fermented liquid and finally bottle it in jars sealed with a lump of mud.

The party becomes livelier and livelier. Soon the abundance of food dwindles, and empty wine jugs and beer containers are everywhere. Nefertiti has just finished consuming a whole roast duck herself and is being helped by a slave to wash her hands from a pitcher and basin filled with clean water.

In the early hours of the morning, the guests begin departing. It has been a celebration they will not forget.

As the sun is beginning to take its first peek over the horizon and the Palace is serenely quiet, two lone figures stand together alongside one of the large pillars in the empty hall. Tut's warm lips press against Anie's in a passionate and meaningful expression of love.

"Only three more days and you are mine completely," he murmurs.

Her warm body wants to cling to his as their lips meet again and again. "I love you, Tut." "I love you, Anie." The lovers depart – each returning to their own quarters.

The royal wedding day arrives. The three days after the big celebration are hectic and pass quickly.

Decorations in the great hall need only fresh flowers to replace the wilted ones.

Ay's paraphernalia for the wedding ceremony are placed in readiness at the throne altar.

The Palace kitchen is a busy place, again preparing food for the reception. Wine and beer are being brought from the royal storehouse.

The future bride and groom are busy in each of their private apartments, being dressed and pampered by their servants.

As usual, Nefertiti is with Anie. "Tahlia, help Her Highness into the wedding dress now." At times, Nefertiti can be quite bossy and overbearing.

Tahlia gives her a look of slight disdain, but dutifully does as she is told.

It is Ankhesenamun who gently places her arm around Tahlia's shoulders and gives her a loving hug. "You know how I have always appreciated everything you have done for me." "Now there is something I want to do for you." She hands her a papyrus scroll. "I know that you can not read this. It states that you are no longer a slave — you are free."

Tahlia's eyes fill with warm tears as she holds the small scroll to her breast. "My deepest thanks, but I do not wish to leave you now. If it is all right with you I would like to stay for a while, at least."

"Of course. I do need you, my dear friend."

Nefertiti is a little alarmed at the two young women, but she knows this is one of those times she is better off to say nothing – even if she does not approve. "Anyway," she murmurs to herself, "This is Anie's wedding day and I don't want anything to spoil it."

From the hallway, a light knock is heard. One of the servants disappears through the archway and when she returns she notifies them that a tall man by the name of Anwar wishes to see the Princess.

"Show him in at once," orders the Queen.

A garland of fresh flowers has just been placed on top of Anie's head, framing her delicate features. Her white gown, pleated and tucked under her bosom and reaching to the floor, completes a vision of loveliness. She has just finished outlining her eyes with black kohl and applying green, ground malachite to her eyelids. Those beautiful eyes glance up to his.

"What a fortunate one the new Pharaoh is," he thinks to himself as his heart seems to skip a beat. If necessary, he knows that he could die for this creature if ever the need be. As he stands staring at her, she breaks the silence.

"It's wonderful to see you, Anwar. Please tell me about Tashery. Is she all right? Does she need anything?" The questions tumble from her lips like a bubbly fountain.

"She is just fine — and growing so fast. The wet-nurse is doing a great job. It has been fortunate that I was able to obtain such devoted and wonderful helpers. And they are very trustworthy."

"We will come to see Tashery as soon as possible after the wedding," interrupts Nefertiti.

"That is fine," Anwar replies. As he departs, he looks back over his shoulder and for a moment he thinks he sees a different look in Anie's eyes. "More of a loving look," he muses. It was a look he had never seen before, and it was definitely directed toward him. But he knows that she loves another. He must be wrong. It must have been a grateful look for all that he has been doing to protect her daughter. As Anwar walks down the long corridor to the reception hall for the wedding, he is thinking that the only happiness he can expect now is in the help of raising and loving a part of her — the little babe Tashery.

As Anwar turns a corner at the end of the long corridor, the groom and his attendants are making their way toward the great hall. As soon as Tut sees Anwar he beckons him to approach the royal party. Anwar, being unaccustomed to thinking of Tut in such an exalted position, bows awkwardly and moves forward.

Tut, seeing the uneasiness, attempts to put him at ease.

"I have missed you very much, not only as the good tutor you are, but as a friend. I'm glad you can attend the wedding."

"I miss everyone, Your Highness, but, as you know, my life has changed and I am enjoying a new position as head tutor for the scribes in a very small but nice village. It is indeed unlike Thebes, but that is what I desire."

"Happiness is what I sincerely want for you, Anwar." "The best of luck to you in your endeavors. You know you are always welcome here at the Palace any time. How very nice to see you again. We must hasten now to the big event — might get in trouble if I hold up my own wedding." A grinning and happy young man bids a fond farewell. He departs quickly.

Anwar continues on his way and enters at the appropriate doorway for guests. After seeing how happy both the bride and groom are, he feels somewhat better. But as the ceremony begins, he stands quietly in a corner of the huge room, a sad and lonely spectator.

The ceremony is brief. An attendant lifts the garland of flowers from Ankhesenamun's head and then Ay places her new crown upon her head.

Tutankhamun stands next to her, holding her hand. As they repeat their vows, they gaze into each other's eyes.

Happiness floods the huge throng like an ocean wave.

In grand unison, everyone bids happiness to the couple — the new King and Queen of Upper and Lower Egypt.

10

THE REIGN

Tomb-like silence sweeps throughout the Palace the day after the wedding celebration. Even the domestic animals seem to sense the welcome change as they lie quietly on their own special mats in designated places about the palace. The usual bustling appearance of Nefertiti darting about is absent as she has left to visit an ailing Queen Tiyi.

Tutankhamun and Ankhesenamun are alone in the Pharaoh's suite and strict orders have been left that no one is to disturb them for any reason whatsoever. Noon fast approaches as the bright new day has appeared and made itself present for several hours.

The two young figures are still in the large bed wrapped in each other's arms. During the long hours spent together their bodies had become one, each giving and taking of one another with all their physical being. Their intimate lovemaking has climaxed the yearning and anticipated passion they both so desired.

"I suppose we should be getting up," she sighs dreamily.

"I'm hungry now," the new young Pharaoh states with a contented and happy lilt to his voice. "Shall I beckon the servants and have them bring us some food?"

"Hold me just a little longer." Anie does not want the magic moments to end. But she tells herself that, as in all good things, the end must come — always too soon.

More caressing and words of sweet endearment follow until what seems a long time later, the couple decides to arise and face the remainder of the short day. The spell is finally broken.

As if a silent signal has been given that goes through the walls and corridors, the whole palace begins to come alive like a giant awakening from a peaceful sleep. Servants emerge like ants in great numbers scurrying about performing their assigned tasks.

The young Queen is led back to her own rooms. Her status has changed so now she enters the privacy of newly decorated and expanded quarters. And Tahlia, with her newly proclaimed and official status of non-slave, waits patiently in the center of the room. As the big double doors are opened for the Queen's entrance, she sees her devoted friend.

"Oh Tahlia," she cries as she runs to the smiling young black woman. "It was all so wonderful! I have so much to tell you." She sighs, and continues: "The King — that sounds strange, doesn't it? — is busy this afternoon so we can have a nice long visit. Is that all right with you?"

Now Tahlia is giving orders to the servants as she is permitted to do with her new status, but she enjoys assisting the new Queen herself. Habits of so long a time are not easily broken.

"That sounds wonderful," replies an enthusiastic Tahlia, as she supervises with the change in dressing. The gown is lifted gently over Anie's head and is pulled down over her slender body. Intricate embroidery has been worked into the pale blue linen gown across the front and the long skirt falls in a mass of pleated folds. Only the very wealthy and members of the royal family possess embroidery work and even then the pieces are preserved as heirlooms and passed from one generation to another. Brightly colored ribbons are tied around the tiny waist and more added to the mop of long black wavy hair.

"No, I won't need that today," Ankhesenamun says as she waves one of the servants away. It is a semicircular kerchief worn under a wig. When used, it is tied by the corners at the nape of the neck under the hair and is to protect the wig on a dusty day.

"I am glad I don't have to wear one of those awful wigs today. I find them so very uncomfortable with all of those curls and braids set with beeswax. My own hair is so long and thick that I only wear the wig for special occasions, and then not always, as Tut prefers me with my own hair."

"You really don't need a wig, Your Highness."

"I want you to call me Anie."

"I don't know if I will be able to, but I shall try... Anie." It is difficult for Tahlia to adjust.

"I hope Mother is having a nice visit with Tiyi. What a shame that Tiyi could not attend the celebrations — her health is not very good and she is getting on in years."

The servants finish their duties and Ankhesenamun waves them from the room.

"Now we can talk in private. As soon as Mother returns, we are planning a trip to see Meri and Tashery. Do you wish to come with us?"

Tahlia replies promptly even though she is not

that fond of Nefertiti: "Yes, I would like to go very much. My plans to leave are not yet complete and I would especially like to see the baby. I'm not sure if I want to see Meri in such a mental state, but I shall accompany you."

The two young women continue their hushed talking, telling each other intimate things that only good friends discuss.

Meanwhile in Tutankhamun's quarters he is assisted with his bath and dressed in royal finery appropriate for the meeting he is to attend.

Ay has made the arrangements for this first important meeting to be held in the Reception Hall. Many of the most prominent figures in Egypt are to welcome their new Pharaoh. But it is Ay who runs everything and all accede to his orders. He is a truly respected man.

In full regalia, the stage is set. The high officials from every district are ushered in, taking their proper places. There are administrators of temples, priests, scribes and civil servants — also a minister of war. As the young King sits on his throne, his grandfather Ay begins speaking:

"As you know, I will brief our new Pharaoh Tutankhamun each morning on all aspects of the Egyptian Kingdom. Heads of all states will report to me daily."

There is nodded agreement throughout the large hall as they know the young Pharaoh needs much supervision and information. There are rumbles of dissent from a few as the passion for power always creeps into the thoughts of some, but the High Priest Ay has set the law and no one wants to confront him directly.

"First I want to speak of the religious upheaval that was so prevalent under Akhenaton's rule. He tried very hard to replace the traditional worship of our god Amun with the worship of his Aton cult but, fortunately, that is over now and I am happy to report that Amun is flourishing throughout Egypt more than ever before."

A sound of applause rings out and a look of contentment sweeps over Ay's face.

"Next I must speak of the war situation. We have much to be thankful for since our armies are performing great feats. The expulsion of the Hyksos and the reconquest of Nubia, not to mention the conquest of Palestine and Syria as far as the Euphrates, are laudable events. But you must remember that in Akhenaton's last year it was not well in Syria and Palestine. The Hittites were beginning to extend their hegemony over the principalities of northern Syria while invaders from the Eastern desert harried Egyptian possessions in Palestine. He did little to demonstrate Egypt's might, and those who relied on him as Pharaoh to protect their bases sent letters to him. Unfortunately, he did not answer them. He liked to boast of our conquests, but he was more of a dreamer than a realist. Our prestige in Western Asia showed a sharp decline."

Those present know that of which Ay speaks is true.

"Enough of war. Let us now decide the location of the tomb."

As is the custom, when the new Pharaoh takes office, preparations for his burial tomb are begun. It takes many years to complete the enormous undertaking.

"Not yet!" A voice rings out strongly from the lips of the young King, and a rather startled Ay takes a step backward.

"I am young and there will be many years to work on my tomb. I would rather be a builder like Amenhotep III — the mighty builder of our Temple at Thebes, the additions to Karnak with the beautiful row of stone rams, additional courts and pylons, and the sacred lake dedicated to his wife, Queen Tiyi. He did magnificent things with the great wealth of Egypt."

And then, with a note of authority in his voice, Tutankhamun continues: "I too wish to be a builder. Karnak is my choice for a place to begin by making some additions to that great temple."

From the hushed silence a gradual roar of approval is heard. It starts to ripple throughout the great hall and gradually ends in full-blown applause. Then, like the sound of cymbals clashing, loud voices in shouts of happy agreement ring out.

A rather surprised Ay gathers his wits about him and keeps his mixed feelings under control. On one hand he is proud of Tut, but on the other hand he has been rebuked in front of all to see and hear. Love and envy swirl about in his whole being. In a calm, loud voice he turns to the young King so all can hear and says:

"As you wish, great Pharaoh of Egypt."

Silence now takes its hold over the crowd just as abruptly as the shouting had taken its turn. All understand that an order from the Pharaoh is instant law and even the High Priest can not overrule.

And Tut, knowing what is happening, stands and turns towards his grandfather.

"High Priest Ay, you shall supervise all work on the Temple and all shall be accountable to only you. Your authority will be above reproach — I so declare and order it!"

Again, applause rings out and a satisfied Ay steps down into the multitude of happy spectators.

As all depart, warm words of approval fill Ay's ears. He glances back over his shoulder, and Tut gives him a loving wink.

It is difficult for the newlyweds to part, but Tut knows that Anie must visit Meri. He has been swept up into his new duties and his days are filled with all kinds of appointments and meetings. He wishes they could be together more but for the time being it is impossible.

"When you return there will be more time for just the two of us, I promise. I will make time," he sighs as he hugs her lovingly.

"I understand the chariot races will take place while I am away. I know how you love to participate in them, but they do become very dangerous at times so please be careful." Her thick black lashes sweep upward and reveal troubled eyes. Then a slight twinkle appears. "I want to return to a whole husband," she teases.

"Don't worry. I shall be careful, Anie. I am really looking forward to using my new chariot — it is a beauty! The craftsmen outdid themselves in making this one." With youthful enthusiasm he pulls at her arm. "Come, I want you to see it."

Before the new chariot is taken to the great arena for the races, it has been delivered to the Palace for a special inspection by the Pharaoh. It now stands near the entrance awaiting approval by its honorable owner. It is indeed a beauty to behold. Not only is it well constructed but strong and exceedingly light. It is covered from top to bottom with gold, and every inch has been decorated with embossed patterns and traditional scenes. On the borders and framework are elaborate ornaments and semi-precious stones and polychrome glass encrusted upon the gold casing. The floor consists of a mesh of interlaced leather thongs covered with an animal skin.

There is no seat since the royal charioteer always stands, ready to leap to the ground from the open back and up again whenever it is necessary. Additional ease and comfort is provided to the Egyptian chariots by placing the wheels and axletree as far back as possible.

A beautiful black horse rigged to the chariot moves nervously. His right hoof thumps impatiently signaling that he wants to be on his way. He is decked out in splendor with sumptuous housings, neck coverings and a crest of ostrich feathers fastened to the headstall and bridle.

"It is truly gorgeous, Tut. Your horse looks fit for a King, as he should." She kisses him gently and then walks to the waiting group.

As Anie throws Tut a farewell kiss she is thinking how young and regal he looks.

"Tell mother Nefertiti I send my love."

"I will — and remember — be careful, take care."

Anie and Tahlia are taken to the landing where they are to leave for the trip down the Nile.

Nefertiti's slender figure is silhouetted against the setting sun as she stands motionless on the deck of the royal yacht. Seeing Anie approaching, she starts waving and smiling. She notices Tahlia walking alongside her daughter, rather than behind, as she used to do as a slave. It is difficult for her to accept this new role for Tahlia. She knows she must treat her differently now, even though it will not be easy. Her strong voice calls out to them as they come nearer: "Everything is ready — we leave soon."

When everyone is on board and all is in readiness, Nefertiti starts explaining plans about a visit first to see Meri, then to Elephantine Island and Tashery.

Tahlia interrupts. "I will wait for you on the yacht when we first stop for Meri's visit. I do not wish to see her."

"That is perfectly all right, Tahlia," Nefertiti states haughtily. Keeping her composure, she continues: "It is best that only Anie and I make the visit."

Realizing there may be trouble, Anie changes the subject and asks her mother how Tiyi is coming along, even though she knows her grandmother's health has not improved.

"Not too well," is the expected answer. "I believe it will only be a matter of time. The gods seem bent on destroying her body. And it isn't that I haven't prayed to all of them enough — and I have certainly gone to the Temple many times to ask the gods to take care of her. There is nothing more I can do."

Nefertiti seems somewhat confused about all of her attempts to help Queen Tiyi and is disturbed that even her favorite gods do not bend to her wishes.

Questions flash through Anie's head regarding her Mother's religion, but she knows it is best to keep silent on the touchy issue. She will have enough to do to keep Tahlia and her Mother from getting into heated arguments.

The voyage will be a long one. Anie hopes the end will come soon.

Many days pass while on board the luxurious yacht and no further confrontations arise between Nefertiti and Tahlia.

Anchored near a small village, the yacht sways gently as it tugs against its restraining ropes. The mental institution is located in this village. Just across the water, Elephantine Island can be seen.

After disembarking, the two Queens, accompanied by a handful of royal guards, make their way up a curved road that leads to a private walled home. As they walk, they see clusters of buttercups and yellow daisies dancing in the bright sunlight. A border of cornflowers seem to bow in welcome.

A visit from the royal family to this asylum is a first. A royal member has never been cared for here before. As Anie and Nefertiti enter the small abode, excitement exudes all about them.

Greeting them is an old woman. She grins and shows a toothless mouth. Greedy-looking eyes peer through thin slits and are surrounded by folds of wrinkles. The short, fat body keeps bowing and bending up and down, up and down until short puffs of air erupt from the round red face. The institution is run by this conniving and clever woman. She likes to receive her pay with room and board. Her duties to take care of these feeble-minded people seem to be secondary. And, unfortunately for them, their care is very limited.

Unknown to Nefertiti and Anie, the patients are lucky if they receive enough food to nourish their frail bodies, much less adequate personal care.

As the old woman leads them through a small hallway towards a large bolted door, they can't help noticing that debris of all kinds has been left strung along the way. The walls are in need of a good scrubbing. The woman releases a leather latch and flings the door open.

Anie and Nefertiti both gasp at the same time. The room is overflowing with pitiful-looking people — both men and women, young and old. Some are moving about the room slowly muttering nonsensical words and phrases while others just sit or kneel against the grimy walls. They all seem to be in a crazed state of mind and are dressed in only a simple, short linen cloth, barely covering their thin bodies.

Nefertiti's voice erupts first: "Isn't that Meri over there?"

Anie follows her Mother's gaze. There, huddled like a frightened caged animal in one of the dark corners, is Meri.

"What is that thing on her head?" questions Anie in a rather startled voice.

"It looks like a handkerchief.... yes, it is... but it has knots tied at each corner."

The odd-looking head covering has been placed on top of Meri's head.

Nefertiti's composure returns and her angry voice fills the room. "Take that thing off of her head immediately!" she orders.

"Why do they do that?" Anie asks. As her eyes sweep over the room she sees that many others have the same covering on their heads.

Nefertiti's eyes blaze. "How dare you treat a member of the royal family like that — ridiculing her with that utterly silly covering!"

119

An attendant quickly bends over the cowering form of Meri and pulls the covering off, revealing short, stubby thatches of hair dotting the scaly scalp beneath.

Tears well in Nefertiti's eyes. "Put it back," she sighs. In her heart she knows that this is a hopeless situation. The bruises on Meri's body tell her that beatings have also taken place.

As they turn to leave, Anie asks: "Mother, does she have to stay here?"

"I'm afraid so, Anie. There is no other place for her to go. It breaks my heart, but we must leave her here." Then Nefertiti adds: "I will make sure a full investigation is made about the management. Changes need to be made."

Meri doesn't even know that they had visited her. She does not know that her body is withering away. She is not aware of the frequent beatings. Her mind has ceased to function. There is no hope for her.

The great yacht makes its way across the water toward Elephantine Island where Tashery's secret hiding place awaits their visit.

Surprised faces appear on the single-sail feluccas as the yacht glides by them. As soon as they see it is the royal yacht, shouts of welcome and happiness pour from their mouths.

"I'm glad you stayed on board, Tahlia," says Anie after she has told her what she had seen on her visit to see Meri.

"I knew it would be like that. That is why I did not wish to go. I want to remember Meri the way she used to be," states Tahlia sadly.

"Mother says she must stay there, but it grieves me that she has to be in that awful place."

"Your Mother is right. It would be worse if Meri lived in the Palace. She would be ridiculed even more and it would be harder on the whole family. At least the only comfort I can offer to you now is that Meri knows nothing of what is going on about her."

Anie knows that Tahlia and her Mother are right and tries to put the sad memory of Meri from her mind.

The island appears before them. Anie's anticipation of getting to see Tashery melts away the sad thoughts of her sister Meri. Now all she can think of is holding her precious baby in her arms once again. Her eyes search for Anwar.

On the welcoming shore stands a tall and handsome man. His dark eyes twinkle as they also search for hers. She walks down the wooden plank toward him and mutual grins of welcome prevail.

Anwar's first impulse is to run and sweep Anie into his arms, but he knows that it cannot be. She belongs to another.

"Anwar!" Anie calls out. Running to him she too wishes that he could hold her, but she realizes her position and wants to be faithful to her husband. She holds herself aloof and acts the part of Queen of Egypt.

"Where is she?" "Oh, I can hardly wait to see her." Anie's steps quicken as she gets closer and closer to Anwar.

Tahlia is having a difficult time keeping up with her, as well as the servants and body guards hurrying behind her. Even Nefertiti is having trouble coaxing her group along. She is usually ahead of everyone, but this time she lags far behind.

"Wait for us!" yells Nefertiti, but she might as well have saved her breath as the two distant figures pay no attention to her — they seem to be in a world of their own.

Anwar gently takes Anie's hand and leads her to the narrow street that will take her to Tashery's secret home. Only Nefertiti and Tahlia accompany them after hot protests from the security guards. Nefertiti yells out determined orders in her usual strong voice and reluctantly they obey. She knows they are only trying to do their jobs well by protecting the royal family, but the secret of Tashery must be kept and she fears that already too many may know about her.

The four enter a lovely home after passing through its private gate. The walls circling the beautiful gardens are covered with green vines that make the whole complex cool. The comfortable interior of the home seems to exude contentment and peace.

The intricately carved wooden door is closed behind them. A slightly built older woman, who has greeted them on their arrival, now leads them into a bright sunny room just off of the main sitting room. Her gray-streaked brown hair, brushed back from her thin face, shows slightly at her forehead and on the sides beneath a white linen head covering. Her kind eyes display sincere pleasure as Anwar introduces her to the royal visitors and Tahlia as "Farida."

Entering the room, they see a beautiful little girl sitting on the floor playing with her toys. She looks up at them with wonderment in her eyes. Ankhesenamun moves slowly toward the small child and speaks softly to her: "Tashery, I am your mother." She then leans over and kisses her gently.

Nefertiti stands watching quietly and thinking how her grandchild looks so much like Anie. She is like a miniature carbon copy of her mother with the same features and — the eyes — those extraordinarily gorgeous eyes.

The child pulls away and a hurt look covers Anie's face. Tashery then toddles towards Anwar and Farida.

"It's all right, child, go to your mother," Farida directs in a hushed voice.

"She is already walking," exclaims Nefertiti in a very proud manner. She is extremely bright and advanced for her age, she tells herself with grandmotherly love.

Tahlia enjoys observing the reunion. She is happy for all of them.

Tashery takes a few hesitant steps toward the beautiful lady who has told her that she is her mother, and stretches her small arms up to her. Nefertiti sees Anie's face light up with joy as she pulls the dear one to her.

"I love you," she whispers in her ear. The child puts her hands around Anie's neck and presses a wet mouth on her cheek. The touching event has everyone wiping tears of happiness from their misty eyes.

The afternoon goes quickly — much too quickly for all. Farida supervises refreshments by having the household servants bring in trays of delicacies.

Anwar continually beams with pride whenever Tashery performs in her delightful childish ways. Soon she becomes weary and nap time has been put off too long already. A nursemaid is summoned and the little one is led, objecting all the way, to her nursery. Anwar's private quarters are situated a short distance down the hall from the nursery so he can always be close by in case Tashery needs him. And

Farida's room is directly across from the nursery so she too can keep a watchful eye on the little princess. There is always the fear hovering over them that someone will learn of Tashery's identity and either kidnap her for ransom or harm her for religious reasons — or, unfortunately, both. These are troubled times indeed and the political and religious upheavals of the country continue.

It is time to depart. Even Tahlia hates to leave as she not only has enjoyed watching the others in lively conversations, she has communicated closely with Farida. It seems as though a new friendship has formed. They chat and walk together to the door.

Nefertiti follows closely behind, knowing that Anwar and Anie want to be alone. She does not have to be told that there is a special bond between them.

Anwar stands close to Anie listening carefully to her warm words.

"You know I can never thank you enough for all that you have done and are doing for our country — and me." As she hesitates, she tries not to linger in her gaze on his handsome face. Her eyes try to avert showing the tenderness she feels so deeply for him. "I know Tashery is well cared for and we are fortunate in having Farida help raise my beautiful daughter."

Now it is Anwar's turn to hold back his true emotions. "Yes," he agrees, "Farida is a wonderful person and seems to love the child." Very gently he takes Anie's hand and, trying to keep his eyes focused downwards, he murmurs, "I will do anything to help my beloved country but, more than that, I would lay down my life for you and Tashery."

As Anwar starts to withdraw his warm hand from hers, she carefully catches it in hers and softly squeezes it. "I will never forget this."

Nefertiti can't help overhearing the intimate words. Walking quickly by, she reminds them that they must leave. She is thinking that the situation could develop into a more serious one. She isn't so sure that she wants this to happen; in fact, she is already making mental plans whereby Anie will have trouble visiting here as often as she would like. After all, her special Tut is King of Egypt and she does not wish any scandal to occur during his reign.

Back on the royal yacht, with the Nile providing their safe transportation home to the Palace at Tell El Amarna, Ankhesenamun and Tahlia stand on the deck. The evening sky is letting nature paint wide strips of red across its horizon as if to color the earth for a short time before blackness takes over.

"Oh, Tahlia, isn't she just beautiful!"

Tahlia knows Anie's thoughts are still with Tashery. "Yes," she answers even though it has been more of a statement than a question. Trying not to break the spell, Tahlia realizes she must remind the Queen that her feelings will have to be kept under control, especially for the child's sake. But as she starts to speak, Nefertiti appears.

"Tahlia, I wish to speak to my daughter."

"Yes, Your Highness." Tahlia departs quickly. Nefertiti can never be one of her favorite people, she thinks to herself.

Nefertiti turns to Anie: "I am aware of what you are thinking my dear, but your visits to Tashery will have to be limited."

Anie does not look at her mother. "Please, don't remind me about that now — just let me enjoy my thoughts of Tashery at this moment."

Nefertiti knows this is not the time to preach her well-intentioned instructions and departs to her comfortable canopied quarters for the long night on the yacht.

As Anie stands alone listening to the sound of the steering paddle and occasional noises from the black shore, her thoughts turn from Tashery to the tall, handsome man who is caring for her daughter. Remembering their brief, but tender, farewell, she sighs softly, "Anwar."

11

TRAGEDY STRIKES

Slate gray skies form a backdrop for the figure of a young man standing straight and rigid on the hillside near the muddy shore. His long colorful flowing robe ripples softly in the invisible breeze. His neck is tiring from the weight of the heavy gold crown that stands high on his head.

As the royal yacht comes into view, he forgets his official status for a moment and, in youthful excitement, the flail he holds in his right hand drops to the ground. There are many servants present and one of them rushes to pick it up for him.

Shouts of welcome can be heard from the large crowd that has gathered to see and welcome the royal family. Eager eyes search the large yacht for the first glimpse of the two Queens. The people love their new young Pharaoh and his wife, Ankhesenamun. Nefertiti is still a favorite, especially since she supports the more popular Amun religion.

Tahlia is at Anie's side as the yacht pushes its way towards the dock. "There he is — over there on that hill," she shouts, pointing to Tutankhamun.

"I see him, Tahlia," replies Anie. How awkward he looks, she thinks to herself, as she sees him drop the flail. She is trying hard to keep thoughts of Anwar from her mind, but she knows that she is comparing his mature years to her husband's younger age. Trying to blank out her thoughts of Anwar, she tries to convince herself that it is Tut who needs her so much.

Gazing up at the young Pharaoh, Tahlia asks: "What is that on his cheek?"

"It looks like a white linen bandage," replies Anie. Then she gasps, "I hope he is all right."

The yacht, now readied for their disembarkation, could not have arrived at a better time. Worried thoughts swirl about in her head.

"I am sure he is fine," assures Tahlia.

They rush to meet him. Anie hastens as fast as her legs will allow.

"Anie, I missed you — it's so good to see you!" A happy Tut coos as he kisses his wife gently but firmly on her eager lips.

"What is wrong with your cheek?" Anxious words pour from the beautiful mouth.

"Not much, Anie. Please don't worry. I received a cut in the chariot races. The physicians took care of it, but they say I may have a scar."

"Oh Tut, I knew those chariot races would be dangerous. How did it happen?"

"One of the wheels hit a rock. I lost control when the horse reared up and I was flung through the air, landing on a sharp object. Other than a few bruises and the cut on my face, I'm fine."

Nefertiti appears, puffing air through tired lungs. "You must be more careful," she scolds. Happy that he has not been injured more seriously, she hugs him warmly.

Turning to Nefertiti, he asks: "Are you coming to the Palace with us,?"

"No," she replies, "I must go to visit Tiyi at Memphis."

"Grandfather Ay says to tell you he is sorry that he is unable to come and welcome you but he has been very busy. He helps me immensely and takes care of many important details that are too much for me." Tut waves a loving farewell to Nefertiti as Anie rushes to embrace her.

Nefertiti hates to leave her loved ones and would really rather go with them, but she knows that Tiyi needs her attention now. She also knows that Ay is keeping a watchful eye on matters.

The crowd disperses quickly, much to the delight of the young King and Queen. Shortly thereafter they find themselves alone at last in the sumptuous living quarters in the great palace at Tell El Amarna.

Anie is happy to be home and anxious to relate the sad situation about Meri. She hates not being able to tell Tut about Tashery and the visit to her secret home, but she has decided it is not necessary to burden him with all of her problems. Also, she would have to include Anwar and somehow she is not too sure if Tut would understand.

"I shall issue orders as soon as possible to improve the living conditions at the asylum where Meri is confined," Tut remarks in a serious manner. "There is no reason why a member of the royal family must be kept like that — it grieves me."

Anie is pleased with his understanding and compassion. She almost blurts out about Tashery, but just then he lifts the bandage from his face and reveals the deep, red scar.

"Oh Tut, that really is a bad cut!"

"Yes, Anie, but I am still going to ride my chariot;

in fact, I am going quail hunting tomorrow." He pauses a moment thinking she might object to his plans but, instead, a wry smile creeps over her face.

"I have something to tell you," she purrs. "I am with child."

Tut's face beams as he pulls her toward him. The warm young bodies meet as she snuggles her head into the hollow of his welcome shoulder.

"Oh Anie, what wonderful news!"

And as the excitement of the moment is experienced they are swept up into a wave of happiness.

At Memphis, hearing the wonderful news of an expected heir to the throne, it is Nefertiti's turn to express her great pleasure. Before anyone else can make a formal announcement, she sends the message throughout all of upper and lower Egypt, sweeping the land like a raging fire out of control. She has contacts everywhere keeping her informed of everything important that takes place so she in turn can relay the messages both going and coming.

After first informing Tiyi of the wonderful news, her daily agenda becomes filled with making arrangements for special thanks to the gods and numerous visits to the temples. Her dead husband's Aton cult has been practically erased throughout the land because of the opposition of both Ay and herself.

Tiyi rallies for a while with the happy news of the forthcoming birth, but her days are numbered and she realizes it. She only hopes that she can live long enough to see her second great-grandchild since she was denied the opportunity to be with Tashery.

Nefertiti finds it difficult to leave, but she hastily returns to Tell El Amarna.

Tahlia is also overcome by the wonderful news. It is as though she is looking for any kind of an excuse just to be with Ankhesenamun.

Abdul, the large handsome black Nubian slave working in the palace kitchen, has tried to win Tahlia's heart, but she does not love him completely. After asking for her hand in marriage, and being refused twice, he becomes discouraged and marries someone else. Tahlia is hurt for a while, but now seems more content than ever to lead a life of love and devotion to her Queen. She feels that she has gained station in her life by being a free person and now any decisions she makes are of her own choosing. Abdul will always remain in her thoughts.

Tahlia can hardly wait for the pending birth of the baby.

Months pass with busy days. Between matters of state and social functions the young Pharaoh has a schedule that fills most of his waking hours. He tires easily and coughing spasms plague him. Secretly, he notices blood in some of his sputum.

Whenever Tut starts to complain, either Grandfather Ay or Nefertiti is always on hand to remind him of his responsibilities for the good of Egypt.

Tut dearly loves his ventures to the marshes for hunting of the various birds. The sound of his arrow striking its target with an abrupt thud is a thrilling experience. But, with the heavy schedule, this favorite sport becomes rarer and rarer as time goes by.

He also wants to be with his wife more, especially in her condition as the birth time nears and she is becoming uncomfortable with the baby growing inside her.

So it is Tahlia again who is always at Ankhesenamun's side when she is in need of companionship. Often they find themselves visiting with one another in the sumptuous royal quarters. As the Queen rests leisurely on one of the sofas, Tahlia plumps the pillows up about her to take the strain off her tired back.

"I love this room, Tahlia." Her eyes dart about looking at all of the objects placed in their own special niches.

"We have received so many beautiful gifts throughout the years."

Tahlia nods in agreement.

"One of my favorites is that lovely floral-design alabaster lamp. When the wick is burning you can actually see figures inside." Wanting to get a closer look, Anie pushes herself up from the sofa and starts toward the table holding the lamp. Moving quickly, she does not see a small stool sitting precariously in her path. A scream fills the room as she goes tumbling over it. She feels a sharp pain, then a rush of warmth between her legs. Tahlia is at her side immediately.

"Get the doctor!" "Quickly, Tahlia!"

The long hours pass slowly. Pale and drained of her energy, Anie sits propped up in her royal bed.

"I lost the baby, didn't I?" Anie's soft voice is filled with remorse.

Tut had been summoned immediately and is at her side. He holds her hand and gently consoles her. "Don't worry, my love, we shall have another baby." "The main thing now is for you to get well."

"Oh Tut, I am so sorry. I wanted to give you an heir to the throne."

"Stop worrying."

Through misty eyes she can't help noticing how ill he looks. "Are you all right?" she asks.

"Yes." "Now get some sleep." "Your mother is on her way."

"That's wonderful. I want to see her very much." Heavy eyelids close engulfing her in welcome sleep.

Anie bounces back from her miscarriage quickly with frequent visits by Nefertiti. Always supportive, Tahlia is there for her.

But it is Tut for whom everyone is concerned. He and Anie are determined to have another baby and, even though his health deteriorates year after year, they succeed. Happily, Anie is pregnant again.

Once again everyone is thrilled with the news and Nefertiti plays the announcer of good tidings.

The happiness is short-lived. The Pharaoh can no longer control his coughing. In a final expulsion of phlegm and blood, the hemorrhaging can not be controlled.

Tut dies in Anie's arm.

His final words to her are: "Like the beautiful flowers along its banks, you are and always will be my FLOWER OF THE NILE."

12

THE PLAN

The sorrow of losing Tut is too much for Anie and, once again, her body expels the unborn child.

There is no heir to the throne of Egypt.

Gloom engulfs the palace at Tell El Amarna. At first, disbelief fills the air as the news of King Tutankhamun's death is announced. Then soft mournful cries come from every room and hallway as the ripple of shock advances like a cold, bitter wind.

Chores are set aside. Kitchen servants are not preparing meals, and soiled linens are left in scrambled piles. Bleating animals are wondering why no one has come to care for them.

A pale and anguished Anie lies in her bed chamber, her dark hair spilling over the soft pillows that Tahlia is plumping about her.

"You must rest," coaxes Tahlia.

Anie gives her a limp smile. "I must see mother and grandfather right away." She hesitates. "I know they are waiting in the next room."

Tahlia knows it is to no avail to argue with her so she starts toward the door. She shakes her head. It is hard to believe that so much has happened in such a short time — such sad happenings.

Nefertiti rushes into the room with Ay at her heels. They are both concerned about Anie's health, but the doctors have assured them that she is recovering nicely from her second miscarriage.

It is Ay who starts talking about all the work that is cut out for him as High Priest. Besides organizing the committees for the long and tedious burial procedures, it is his responsibility to arrange new leadership for the country. As of this moment, there is no ruler of Egypt. He begins explaining that, even though Anie has the title as Queen of Egypt, she does not have the power thereof. She must remarry as soon as Tut is buried. The one she marries will be be King of Egypt and ruler.

Nefertiti gives him a disputing glare. "Why can't Anie be Queen and ruler?"

Ay replies angrily: "A man must be Pharaoh!"

"Not so!" yells Nefertiti. "You are forgetting there was a female ruler by the name of Hatshepsut who reigned earlier. She had the full power of a Pharaoh. And I would like to add that she devoted herself to the administration and the encouragement of commerce."

"Are you sure she was a woman?" Ay retorts. "I know of whom you speak, but the pictures of her chiseled on tomb walls show her with a beard."

"That's not fair!" "You know that was a false beard. Men can not accept the fact that a woman can do a good job as a ruler of a country as well as they can."

Nefertiti knows it is useless to continue the argument. She also knows that Ay is very powerful.

Leaning toward Anie, Ay says gently: "For the good of Egypt, you must make definite plans to remarry." He adds: "Perhaps you would consider marring me."

Both Anie and her mother are stunned.

Hastily he adds: "Of course, it would be in name only. I love you Anie — only as a grandfather loves his granddaughter." His eyes soften and Anie knows he is telling the truth.

"I have seventy days to make a decision. It will be mine alone, grandfather."

Tahlia stands and reminds them that Anie must get some rest.

Nefertiti has never accepted the fact that Tahlia is a friend and not a slave, but looking at her daughter she knows Tahlia is right. She and Ay leave quickly.

As soon as they depart, Anie turns to Tahlia and tells her to beckon a scribe. When Tahlia starts to oppose the request, it is Anie who gets out of bed and pushes her out of the door.

"Hurry, Tahlia, time is of the essence!" "Don't worry, I feel fine."

Tahlia returns shortly with a scribe at her elbow. Anie motions him to the writing table.

The scribe holds a piece of papyrus in his left hand, and his right hand is poised with a reed pen.

"Anie begins dictating a letter as he dips the pen into a small jar of paint: "This is to the Hittite Prince, Shubbuliliuma." Then she continues: "I wish to share my throne with you, but the union must take place in exactly seventy days. If it does not, all will be lost. If I do not hear from you within that time, I will understand that you are not interested."

"I desire that this be carried to the Hittites' palace at once. I want to emphasize the fact that this is to be kept in the most strict confidence."

The scribe rolls the papyrus and ties it. Anie extends her hand to him so that the seal from her royal ring can be used to authenticate the document.

After applying fresh wax to the scroll, he presses the ring against it. Tucking it it securely under his arm, the scribe bows and makes a hasty departure.

Tears run down Anie's cheeks. "I don't even know that prince, Tahlia, but I am trying to do what is best for Egypt. That is what Tut would want me to do, don't you think?" She turns to her loyal and trusted friend for support.

"Follow your heart — that is what your husband would want."

"I am not sure about grandfather Ay. Maybe he is right about the throne," sighs Anie. Then her thoughts turn to Tashery and Anwar and she wonders how they are.

Days later at Elephantine Island, the sad news has spread and Anwar and his household have been informed. Tashery is nine years old now and comprehends the significance only to a point. Being kept away and in secret all these years she never knew the king. Ankhesenamun visited often enough for her to know that she is her mother, but she is very close to Farida who treats her like her own daughter.

Anwar, in Tashery's eyes, is the only father she has known. He is always there when she needs him and he makes sure that she is raised properly. He has grown to love her as if she were his own daughter.

Anwar had met other women and at one time had considered marriage, but when the time came for the important decision, it was always Anie he thought about and loved so much. Also, he is not an Amun follower. He believes that now the time has come, fate showing its hand, to prove that the Egyptian gods are powerless or non-existent. Perhaps Akhenaton was right in believing in one all powerful god. Being an exceptional person in handling details and accomplishing what he goes after, wheels in his head begin spinning. He calls his household staff together and explains a complicated and ever-so-secret plan involving Tashery. They have been used to protecting her over the years so they are not alarmed.

With final instruction to Farida, Anwar leaves quickly for Tell El Amarna. He must receive Anie's approval before putting his plans into motion.

When Anie hears of his visit, she is overwhelmed. Alone in her private sitting room, the door opens and he enters. He closes the door gently behind him and looks directly at her. He can't believe how beautiful she looks, even more than he had remembered. Without hesitation, Anie runs to him stretching her arms up and around his neck, all the while sobbing and telling him in disjointed sentences all that has happened.

A flood of emotion overtakes Anwar and his strong arms fold around her drawing her close to his warm body. She welcomes his reaction and they are both caught up in the enchanted moment. Cares seem to float into nothingless as the two lovers' lips meet for the first time. The thrill and excitement continues as one kiss leads to another and their passions become almost uncontrollable.

"Oh Anie, I love you so much and need you," he says huskily.

"I love you, Anwar." She pulls him back to her. "I loved Tut too... he was ill for such a long time..." She hesitates and then asks, "How is Tashery?"

"Please, you don't have to explain anything about Tut. Tut is gone... and Tashery is just fine." Then he adds, "You have a right to a new life."

He takes her hand and leads her to a sofa. "Now listen carefully. I want you to understand what I am saying." His eyes become intent. "I have heard there are distant lands — unexplored territories that are far, far away. They can be reached by the great body of water into which the Nile flows. Foreigners have traveled from other places to Egypt from countries using that sea, but the land of which I speak is much farther away. And there is also another sea beyond the first one. It is rumored that only water is seen for many, many days. It could become very dangerous." He adds: "Have you heard any of these stories?"

Nodding yes, she urges him to tell her more.

"Since our sailing vessels have already proven that they can endure long distances, I have a plan to equip a large one and take you and Tashery out of Egypt to a place of safety. I wish I could guarantee where it would be. The second sea that we would have to cross is unexplored."

Anie is a little astounded at the thought of the uncertain destination and the danger involved, but, as she listens to Anwar, she knows one thing for sure that she wants to be with him and Tashery... and safe.

"If Tashery is not protected, she could be destroyed in the revolution that is surely coming — and soon. If certain ones knew that Akhenaton had fathered her, and she is one of his three surviving blood kin, she could be put on the throne and used as a puppet. No telling what they would put the poor child through. In all probability, they would use her for their own selfish greed and then kill her."

Anie sighs, and nods her head in agreement.

Anwar puts his hand under her chin and says slowly: "I want to marry you, Anie. I want Tashery to be my daughter."

"I want to marry you, Anwar, but Ay has suggested that I marry him — in name only, of course—for the sake of Egypt."

"I shall talk to him. Maybe a way can be devised to satisfy all. In the meantime, I have many people to see and many arrangements to make in Thebes."

He stands to leave and then bends down to kiss her warmly. "Don't worry. All will be well." "The plan must... will... succeed!"

Anwar departs for Thebes.

Thebes is a bustling city. Upon hearing of the death of the Pharaoh, the businessmen begin checking their inventories. Their street-lined shops will be selling all kinds of wares associated with the preparation and burial. Hundreds of items from Egyptian jewelers, leather workers, cabinet makers, weavers, potters, etc., will be needed.

A royal goldsmith has already begun work on a special gold mask that will adorn the mummy's face.

A pleasant odor reaches Anwar as he enters the city. Fresh bread is being baked in front of one of the shops.

People are everywhere. Hundreds of donkey carts fill the roads, some piled high with their precious cargos.

Anwar manages to make his way to a guest house where he unpacks in his room and starts implementing his plans.

13

THE MUMMY

The body of the dead sovereign, Tutankhamun, has been taken into the city of Thebes to the embalming workshop. The sign on the door reads, "House of Vigor." Here the process of embalming called "senefer," (restoration of vigor)," is being performed.

The corpse is lifted carefully upon a stone table. Making a long incision on the left side of the abdomen, the embalmer removes the vital organs. Each organ is rinsed in palm wine and spices to sweeten it, and then placed in natron. Only the heart is left in the body.

The abdomen is also washed out with palm wine and with an infusion of pounded spices. After that it is filled with crushed myrrh, cassia and other aromatic substances.

To help speed up the drying process and also to prevent accidental crushing disfigurement, rags, straw, wood shavings, and sand dried grass and linen bags filled with natron are available to be used for stuffing.

After the stuffing is completed, the embalmer sews the incision together.

A metal hook is used to extract the brain through the nostrils, and the fragments are thrown away. The embalmer then dissolves what is left in the skull with aromatic lotions.

Finally, the corpse is transferred to a low stone table which slopes slightly from head to foot to permit drainage. Generous quantities of natron are heaped over the body to remove all moisture. This drying out process will take forty days.

And now the forty days have passed. To extend the drying out process longer is pointless and, indeed, might do harm to the mummy itself.

Hordes of people swarm about the entrance of the "House of Vigor." Many accomplished artists and skilled craftsmen arrive and enter the workshop. They leave their precious works for their beloved deceased Pharaoh and depart in a solemn mood.

Then the delegation of a dozen or more priests and technicians arrive. Each one will have a special task to perform. The last to enter the dark doorway is the High Priest Ay.

The room is dim and foreboding with its barren walls and cold stone floor. Wooden chests with open lids line one side of the room. They are filled with essential supplies. In one corner the light from an oil lamp glistens brightly and reveals a large magnificent gold coffin. It rests on a wooden sledge.

Two stone tables occupy the center of the room. The first table was used for body preparation, and a second sloping table holds the natron-covered corpse.

Nearby, a beautiful elevated bed is being prepared for the final mummification procedures. The bed is gilded, with carved lion figures on its four sides. An occasional flicker from a lamp makes the dark, haunting eyes of the lion glisten as if it is alive.

Painstakingly, the natron is removed and the body cleansed. Two embalmers gently lift and place the mummy on the bed.

The cleaning and anointing of the corpse, the wrapping of all the items, as well as all of the necessary religious recitations, will take an additional thirty days.

The specific time in the embalming workshop is seventy days. This seventy-day mummification process has significance in Egyptian religion. This is the exact period of time that the dog star Sirius disappears from the heavens and then reappears.

As the star "dies" and is "reborn" after seventy days, so the dead – after a similar period – are ready for rebirth in the other world.

Ay is making a quick check to see if everything is in readiness. Placed on one of the tables is an array of clay jugs and bottles holding liquid unguents. These ointments will be used lavishly as part of the burial ritual for the consecration of the dead king before his entrance into the presence of the great god Osiris of the Underworld. Jewelry, personal items, emblems, amulets are all in readiness.

An awe-inspiring burnished gold mask, in the likeness of the king, has been placed on the table next to a large heap of very fine linen cut in long strips. Some are as long as forty-nine feet and up to eight inches wide. There is also padding, shaped wadding and folded materials.

A tear runs down Ay's cheek as he see the gold mask. The beautiful and unique specimen bears the portraiture of a sad but calm youth overtaken prematurely by death.

"Eighteen years of life seems to be an unfair length of time," sighs Ay.

On the forehead of the mask, wrought in gold, are the royal insignia – the Nekhebet vulture and the Buto Serpent – emblems of the two kingdoms over which he reigned, Upper and Lower Egypt respectively.

A conventional Osiride beard is attached to the chin of the mask, and is wrought in gold and lapis lazuli colored glass. Glass objects, and objects adorned with glass, are considered very valuable.

Next to the mask on the table lies one of the finest ornaments of all. It is a small pectoral – an ornament worn on the breast – fashioned to represent a seated vulture. Inlaid with green glass, lapis lazuli and carnelian it is intended to symbolize the southern goddess Nekhebet of El Kab. It is an exquisite example of a goldsmith's work. The characteristics of the bird are those of the sociable vulture which is identical to the vulture insignia of Upper Egypt. The clasp of the suspending straps takes the form of two miniature hawks. Under the pectoral itself – around the neck of the bird goddess – a tiny pectoral is represented in the form of the king's cartouche.

A pile of stone scarabs await their use. These "beetles" have a religious connection with the solar and lunar disks they hold in their forelegs. The lunar disk symbolizes the god Thoth who personifies the moon. Both disks are in great part the original sources of Egyptian mythology and the sun is a sacred symbol with the living, but even more with the dead.

On some of the scarabs, inscribed on their bellies, are prayers for the dead Pharaoh and are sent by relatives and friends — some messages of condolence for the family of the deceased. Others have magical formulas inscribed on them to help the deceased through the Underworld.

Oil-burning lamps in the room are not giving enough light so Ay moves one of the many copper shields positioned around the room. This will better reflect the light from the sun which is shining through the clerestory windows.

A colored stone, in the center of Ay's high head piece, dances in the welcome light. Gray hair at his temples frame the thin, pleasant-looking face. Deep lines show determination and knowledge. When no one is looking, he snuffs out one of the incense burners as the pungent smoke is causing his eyes to burn. Even though the incense is of religious significance, it is more than he can bear.

Ay, as the "Official of the Secret of the Embalming Workshop," signals to begin.

Standing next to him is the "Reader" priest who is to supervise the work and recite the appropriate formulas.

Assisting with the 143 objects that are to be wrapped in the mummy is the "Embalmer of Anubis," dressed as the black god and wearing a jackal headpiece. His eyes squint through the small openings of the mask.

The "Chancellors of the God" priest chants and recites appropriate religious verses and instructions from the "Book of the Dead."

There are four small coffinettes of beaten gold which are 1 ft. and 3-3/8 in. high, each sitting side by side on the table. They are inlaid in a feathered pattern (rishi) with colored glass and carnelian.

The dead king's viscera have dried in the natron for forty days. They are removed and cleansed. All is in readiness. The appropriate protecting gods' and goddesses' names are inlaid on top of the containers. Each organ is placed inside accordingly. There are also mini-gods – "Sons of Horus" – indicative of each organ.

The liver is placed in the first coffinette. Isis, the human-headed goddess, is its representative as well as "Imsety" its mini-god.

The second coffinette now holds the lungs, represented by the goddess Nephthys and the mini-god "Hapy."

Lifting the stomach, it is arranged in the third coffinette and has a jackal goddess, Neith. Its mini-god is "Duamutef."

Fourth and last coffinette contains the intestines. A falcon goddess, Selkit, is its representative, and the mini-god is "Qebhsenuef."

These four coffinettes will be placed later in a beautiful canopic chest for inclusion in one of the four rooms of the tomb.

A technician notes that the head of the dead king is very broad and flat-topped with a markedly projecting occipital region. The general shape of the head is like that of his deceased father and former ruler of Egypt, Akhenaton.

"Yes," replies Ay, "It is a family resemblance and is a very uncommon type."

A skull cap is placed on the head. A long piece of narrow linen is then lifted from the table and gently wrapped around the head. A magnificent crown is positioned on top which encircles the head.

The exquisite pectoral ornament Ay noted before is now hung over the upper part of the chest and around the neck by means of lapis lazuli and gold flexible straps.

Another pectoral ornament is placed still lower on the chest in the form of three scarabs, made of lapis lazuli, supporting a symbol of heaven – disks of the sun and moon. Their posterior legs hold the Neb emblem of sovereignty upon a horizontal bar from which marguerites have been applied and lotus flowers hang.

Twenty amulets are grouped and two kinds of symbolic collars are arranged between six layers of linen bandages. A breast plate in chased sheet gold covers the neck and forms the uppermost layer.

This profusion of amulets and sacred symbols placed on the neck and head are of extreme significance. They suggest how greatly the dangers of the Underworld are feared by the dead.

The "Reader" priest recites more verses from "The Book of the Dead" in a low, quiet voice.

Included in the wrappings are two groups of finger rings – one group of five over the wrist of the right hand, and beside the wrist of the left hand a group of eight rings. These are made of massive gold, lapis lazuli, cloudy-white and green chalcedony, turquoise – and one of black resin.

Both forearms are smothered from elbow to wrist with magnificent bracelets; seven on the right and six on the left. They have granular gold-work, open-work carnelian plaques and rich gold and electrum work. Wrist-bands have flexible beadwork, and others with elaborate geometric and floral designs, inlaid with semi-precious stones and polychrome glass.

Each finger and thumb on both hands are wrapped in more fine strips of linen. Then each is enclosed in a gold sheath. Gold rings are then placed on the second and third fingers.

Amulets, a gold girdle, a blue faience collar made up of minute beads – and a dagger – a total of ten items – are wrapped in the abdomen. A ceremonial apron is placed over this.

Between the legs, seven golden plates are wrapped in the bandages, and another fine and unique dagger, housed in a gold scabbard, is also included.

The two daggers were among Tut's prized possessions and a gift from a Hittite Prince. They were made of a strange, hard metal unknown to the Egyptians. These "iron" blades could penetrate materials unfazed by the softer Egyptian knives.

A broad barrel-shaped anklet is tucked in the hollow of the left groin with the royal insignia of the diadem.

Seven circlets and four collarettes of Egyptian cloisonne are placed over the legs.

Gold painted sandals, made of sheet-metal to imitate rush-work, are placed on his feet. Each toe is enclosed in a separate gold stall, having details such as the nails and first joints of the toes engraved upon them. A gold wire bangle is placed around the right ankle.

A priest motions to Ay: "That is the completion of the 143 objects we wish to be included in the mummy, except, of course, the gold mask."

Ay nods in agreement. He is pleased with the wrapping of the personal and religious items that have been carefully placed over the head, neck, thorax, abdomen and limbs of the king.

The personal property consists of the beautiful pectorals, the majority of the rings and bracelets, the daggers and the crown.

For religious purposes, the various collars and amulets of chased sheet-gold, inlaid amulets, bead collarettes, toe and finger stalls, sandals, the apron, symbolic trappings and the gold mask are intended to be of benefit to the Pharaoh.

All of these beautiful objects represent the fine work of the skilled Egyptian craftsmen of Thebes. Technicians in this "House of Vigor" realize the long hours of work and dedication that have gone into each piece of art and admire these craftsmen. They love their Pharaoh Tutankhamun – both in life and in death.

The last and outermost strips of linen covering are placed on the mummy. They are adorned with richly inlaid gold trappings hanging from a large pectral like figure of the Ba bird, representing the soul. Its full-spread wings stretch over the body. The longitudinal bands down the center are made of gold plaques, bearing welcoming speeches of the gods, and held together by threads of beads.

A priest chants:

"The goddess of the sky, Nut, the Divine Mother says: 'I reckon thy beauties, O, Osiris, King Kheperunbre; thy soul livest; thy veins are firm. Thou smellest the air and goest out as a god, going out as Atum, O, Osiris, Tutankhamun. Thou goest out and thou enterest with Ra...' "*The god of the earth, the prince of the gods, Geb, says: 'My beloved son, inheritor of the throne of Osiris, the King Kheperunebre; thy nobility is perfect; thy Royal*

Palace is powerful; thy name is in the mouth of the Rekhyt; thy stability is in the mouth of the living, O, Osiris, King Tutankhamun, thy heart is in thy body eternally. He is before the spirits of the living, like Ra he rests in heaven."

Accompanying the bands along the sides of the mummy, from the shoulders to the feet, are festoons of even more ornate straps attached to the transverse bands. They are made up of elaborate small inlaid gold plaques also threaded together with beads. The devices on these side straps are of geometrical patterns – Ded and Thet symbols, solar uraei and cartouches of the king.

Some of these bands are part of a residue from Smenkhkare's burial. Where his name appears, it is defaced and the bands are reused.

The table is now void of the hundreds of yards of linen that was consumed in the wrapping of the mummy. Only the gold mask remains.

A 296-pound, six foot long, solid gold coffin is dragged on a sledge, supported by casters, from the corner of the room to the side of the bed.

It takes two of the technicians to pull it because of its great weight. Others join them, lining up on each side and, in unison, lift the top off and place it on the floor. Then they gently lift the mummy and lower it into the coffin.

With steady hands, Ay reaches for the gold mask. He carefully holds the treasure and then places it on the mummy, covering its head and shoulders. Ay can't help noticing that the face on the mask looks so much like Akhenaton; and in profile, an even stronger likeness to the Queen Tiyi. Ay's eyes glisten with tears.

A priest begins reciting more verses of religious significance as sweet-smelling oil is poured over the mummy. About a bucketful of this oil has been placed in jugs and bottles and now, one by one, they are used. The priests are very careful not to get any of the liquid unguent on the head or feet of the mummy.

The lid of the coffin is fastened to the shell by means of eight gold tenons, four on each side, and are held in their corresponding sockets by silver nails.

The coffin is now ready to be dragged on the sledge from the "House of Vigor" through the town of Thebes and then to the banks of the Nile. There, a funerary boat awaits to transport it across the river. After it arrives on the other side, it will again be dragged from the riverbank for a distance of five and one-half miles to the Valley of the Kings to the awaiting tomb.

As Ay looks at the closed gold coffin with the carved face of Tutankhamun staring up at him, he makes a solemn vow to himself. He is going to do all that he possibly can to prevent the violation of this mummy – the remains of one whom he loves so much. He realizes that all of the other mummies and their tombs in the Valley of the Kings have been robbed and ravaged in the past – some very soon after their tomb was sealed.

But, this will be different, he swears to himself.

A very stern frown crosses the forehead of Ay.

14

FINAL PREPARATIONS

The seventy days have passed quickly for Anwar. During that time he has made numerous visits to all kinds of suppliers for the cargo to equip his vessel. It has been difficult to keep the secret, but he has done a good job. No one is suspicious since he is not known in Thebes and they think he is just another sea captain replenishing his supplies.

Recruiting a loyal crew has been no problem as there are many who want to escape the unwanted changes in the country.

Anwar's years of training and working as a chief scribe enables him to know how to keep meticulous records and to know what to order and how much to pay. With Anie's wealth, there is no concern what the cost will be — a few gold treasures from the palace will outfit the entire vessel.

From Thebes he sails to Elephantine Island to prepare Tashery and Farida.

On arrival, Tashery is excited over the news that she is to take a long voyage — and with her mother — but Farida is a little hesitant at first. She realizes what a great undertaking it is. After very careful consideration of plans she must make for herself prior to departure, her decision to go is welcomed by all. She loves Tashery as if she were her own child.

"Farida will make a wonderful companion," Anwar states proudly.

And a great undertaking it will be! Anwar again leaves for Thebes. "I will see you soon!" He waves goodbye to Tashery and Farida.

In the meantime, Anie goes to the palace at Memphis. Tiyi's health has not improved. She is gravely ill. Nefertiti is staying with Queen Tiyi.

Anie sits with her mother as they enjoy viewing the manicured gardens of the palace. Little birds are diving down to a pedestaled bowl beneath some trees. They scold and chirp as they fly into the shallow water. Soon they become furry-looking little balls after tossing the water over their tiny heads. Some have finished and are now sitting quietly on a nearby branch, preening and fluffing their clean feathers.

Ani and Nefertiti gaze at one another. Neither wants the time to pass quickly as they both know that this will be one of their last times together. The bond of mother and daughter is special and wonderful. It is Nefertiti who breaks the silence:

"I suppose you are all packed?"

"Yes," replies Anie. "Tahlia and I have been trying not to forget anything. I am limited to one chest for my clothing and personal items. There just isn't going to be much room on the sailing vessel. Everyone must compromise on what they can take."

"I suppose Tahlia is packed also?"

"Not at this time; in fact, I was a little surprised that she hadn't done hers yet. But she has assured me that she has ample time and will be ready."

Nefertiti says nothing but is thinking that it is a little strange that Tahlia would be delaying something so important.

By this time, Anwar has sent news to Anie regarding the final plans. She explains the details to her mother: "After Tut's burial we will cross over to Thebes. Anwar, Tashery, Tahlia, Farida and I will board the ship and sail northward to The Great Sea. Since we will be racing against time, our stop here at Memphis will be brief – a final farewell to you and Tiyi."

"It sounds complicated to me," remarks Nefertiti, "But I know Anwar is a very capable young man and can accomplish this sea voyage."

Nefertiti pauses, and then adds: "Ay's decision for your marriage to him in name only is a an excellent one. Egypt must have a king as soon as possible."

"I am so happy you feel the way you do mother. I love Anwar very much and I believe he loves me — and we both love and adore Tashery."

Tears trickle down a face that usually can stay composed even at stressful times. But the thought of her grandchild Tashery is too much for Nefertiti to bear. She knows she will not have a chance to see her grow up and bloom into womanhood.

Seeing the tears, Anie also cannot restrain herself and they both embrace with loving tenderness.

The visit is ending. Anie must return home.

Nefertiti hands Anie a small box.

"This is a locket of Tiyi's hair. It should be placed in the Treasury Room of Tut's tomb."

"I will see that it is done."

"I love you, my daughter."'

"And I love you too, mother, and I will love you always."

Acting the part of a queen, the part she has played for so many years with Akhenaton, Nefertiti collects herself, straightens her shoulders and sits erect. Her finger rubs a ring that she is wearing on her left hand. The head of a lioness is carved in alabaster depicting the warlike goddess Sekhemet.

"I saw Meri recently and her mental health has not changed."

"Have the conditions where she lives improved as Tut ordered?" Anie asks.

"They seemed better than before, but as long as benefits are so inadequate in a mental institution such as that one, care will never be as good as it should."

Servants bring in refreshments. The aroma of fresh herbs fills the room as steamy curly-cues circle above a hot teapot.

Sipping from one of the gold cups, Anie says: "I want to see grandmother Tiyi before I depart, even though I realize that she may not recognize me."

"'She seems to sleep most of the time. I think she may know me once in a while."

They rise and stroll through the garden and enter Tiyi's living quarters.

Anie leans down and kisses the sweet face. Her grandmother is asleep. A beautifully designed robe covers the frail body. She does not awaken.

"Life can be tragic at times," she whispers to herself.

In the quietness, only the faint sounds of birds splashing in a nearby birdbath can be heard.

Anie returns to Tell El Amarna.

Knowing the urgency for a quick marriage to Ay, she and Tahlia hastily pack for their voyage to Thebes.

Meanwhile, Anwar rushes to Thebes for an all-important meeting with Ay. No one is more aware of the necessity of placing a new Pharaoh on the throne than he. With his and Anie's future hanging in the balance, he hopes upon hope that he can convince Ay of the wisdom of his position.

Upon arrival in Thebes, Anwar finds Ay in the temple at Karnak busy arranging for an elaborate coronation ceremony to follow the funeral.

"I know how much you have to think about and plan, but we must talk."

Ay paces back and forth as he sees the tall slender figure of Anwar in the doorway. He likes what he sees. This is a sincere and courageous man.

"I am happy you have come. We have much to discuss." Ay hesitates; "First, let's talk about Anie."

Anwar nods in agreement. "Yes, she is most important. You know that I love her with all my heart and want to marry her — and take her away."

"She is indeed important and we all love her."

Ay continues:

"I know that she has told you of my plans about marrying her for the good of Egypt." He pauses, and adds: "These are anxious times."

"I believe you should marry her," states Anwar.

Ay is somewhat surprised at Anwar's statement, but is pleased that he understands the situation.

Anwar explains the plan: "A private wedding ceremony for you and Anie can be performed here with just a few in attendance prior to Tut's funeral. In that way Anie and I can leave immediately following the entombment ceremony." "Anie and I shall unite in marriage at a later appropriate time."

"Your plans please me very much," beams Ay. "This will enable me to be the successor to the throne and I will be Pharaoh of Egypt."

"Anie informed me that she sent a message to Shubbuliliuma, the Hittite Prince, requesting that he might share the throne with her for the sake of Egypt, but there has been no response. Of course, it would have been only a temporary solution to the problem. Her plans are to be with me. We want to be together and spend the remainder of our days sharing our lives."

Anwar continues: "I can marry Anie on the vessel as soon as we sail."

"A priest will sail with you," adds Ay. "One of my most honorable ones has told me he wants to go on the voyage. He will be needed for other services as well."

"Are you planning to rule Egypt alone?" asks Anwar.

"Yes," replies Ay.

"By the way, how is Tashery?" "Is she taking this all right?"

"She is a wonderful little girl and is looking forward to being with her mother — and the trip fascinates her." "It will be a very long — and a very difficult one."

Ay looks directly at Anwar. "We must discuss the vessel now. I have decided that you should take the royal yacht."

Anwar is startled by the statement. The royal yacht is more than he had ever dreamed of sailing.

"This is quite generous of you, sir."

"It is the largest in the fleet and you will need the space. The more water jugs and food you can take, the better." "Also, there will be room to erect two shelters on deck rather than just the usual one. In this manner, there will be one shelter for the women and one for the men." The pens for the livestock and poultry below deck can be larger."

Anwar is pleased. "I have already arranged for many large leather containers, bottles and clay jugs. Some will be filled with water and some with wine and precious oils. Meats and fruits are being dried by the bushel. Of course we shall have an ample supply of fresh food, meat and poultry in addition to the live animals and birds. The perishables will be consumed first."

"Supplies will include reed ropes, extra sailing cloth, papyrus and pens for recording our voyage, clothing, bedding, lamps, etc."

A frown crosses Anwar's brow. He continues: "There are islands in the first great body of water on which we will be sailing, but it is the second one that I worry about. Rumor is that a narrow channel separates these two enormous bodies of water and when other sailing vessels have passed this point, they are no longer heard from. That is the part of the journey that concerns me the most. I must try to prepare for the unknown."

Ay nods in agreement. He knows that Anwar speaks the truth.

"You will need special people," says Ay.

"Yes." "I have tried my best to select dedicated workers who are skilled tradesmen and sailors. Some are married and taking their families and others are single men and single women. All will perform multiple tasks. Even Anie will have to help." "We will all have to work hard to survive."

On arrival at Thebes, Anie and Tahlia are met by Anwar and Ay. They are whisked to the Temple at Karnak where Tashery and Farida have arrived from

Elephantine Island and await their presence. Hugs and kisses are hurriedly exchanged.

The wedding consists mainly of signatures applied to papyrus documents and final legal acceptance by the priests.

The new Pharaoh of Upper and Lower Egypt, Ay, is now proclaimed in a brief ceremony. The public coronation will take place after Tut's funeral.

Ay takes Anwar's hand in his and with a warm handshake and embrace, bids him farewell.

As the others depart, Pharaoh Ay stands alone in the great hall. A sadness encompasses him. He knows the events that are to take place will affect and change many lives. He moves toward the sacred alter. "Life is a series of changes," he reflects.

15

VALLEY OF THE KINGS AND THE WREATH OF FLOWERS

It is early morning and already the heat from the sun makes the Valley of the Kings parched and dry. Sandy hills loom barren against the blue horizon looking like sleeping giants. Many man-carved entrances to tombs dot the hillside.

In the bowels of the solid rock, tombs of past Egyptian pharaohs and noblemen lie silent. They have all been stripped of their treasures by tomb robbers, and their mummies violated in every conceivable way.

In a low-lying area near the entrance to the valley, another tomb is being prepared as the final resting place for the young Pharaoh Tutankhamun.

This tomb is small compared to the size of the other pharaohs buried here. It is more like one that a nobleman would have, but due to the urgency of the burial, this is the chosen location.

Great hope is that this small tomb might escape the ravages and greed of the tomb robbers. Only time will tell.

TUTANKHAMUN'S TOMB IN THE VALLEY OF THE KINGS

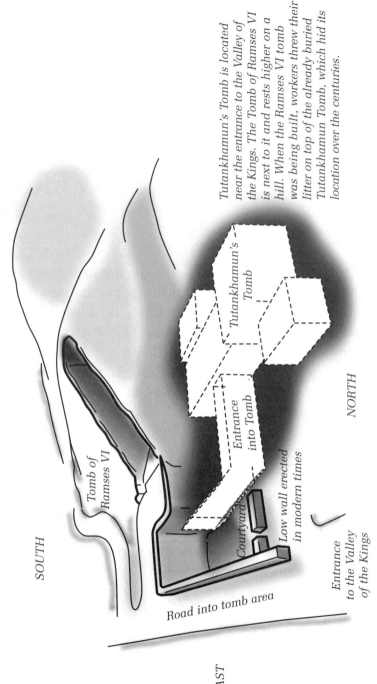

The area is a beehive of activity as caravans of people are arriving from the banks of the Nile five and one-half miles away. Their journey has brought them from the great city of Thebes, the capital of Egypt, situated on the opposite side of the river.

A snake-like line winds as far as the eye can see. Everyone seems to either be carrying, pulling or dragging something. As they move closer to the tomb entrance, it is evident that these are the supplies and treasures that the dead king will need in his afterlife. All are to be placed in his tomb and, hopefully, sealed forever.

Pairs of oxen are quietly pulling large items on sledges or in carts, while snorts and whines of stubbornness and discontent can be heard from heavy-laden donkeys.

Soldiers on horseback ride up and down the long line coaxing the slow-paced to hurry. A tense and sad atmosphere fills the air hanging like an invisible cloud.

The funeral procession arrives at the opening of the tomb. The sun's rays reflect brightly off the surface of a solid gold coffin mounted on a sledge provided with runners. Its tremendous weight is being hauled by a team of forty couriers and officials. Ropes are fastened around their waists, crossed up over their shoulders and attached to the front of the sledge. Taking turns during the long distance from the river has given them some relief, but now their bodies ache from the exhausting task.

The hasty marriage ceremony and crowning of Ay as Pharaoh has not left time to appoint a new High Priest. Ay determines that he will continue in this capacity until his grandson is properly buried.

The mummy of Tutankhamun is in the solid gold coffin. Even though most funerals at this time in Egypt would use oxen to haul the coffin, it is considered a very high honor to be selected to help with this laborious chore for their beloved Pharaoh.

Walking slowly in front is the High Priest Ay. He is attired in a long white flowing robe. A bejeweled collar covers his shoulders. A high, snug-fitting headpiece indicates his important position.

Ay turns and signals to halt. A small ceramic vase is held in his right hand. He tips the vase slowly and begins to pour the sweet-smelling oil over the top of the coffin. All the while he is chanting religious verses to the Sun-god Amun-Ra.

In the middle of one of the verses, a loud and angry shout erupts from the crowd that has gathered around the coffin. "That is enough!"

The serious religious and political upheaval in the country is taking its toll. Other spectators shout additional angry remarks.

Knowingly, Ay finishes the ceremony quickly and motions for the coffin to be taken down into the tomb. With the help of Nubian slaves, they slide the coffin down the sixteen steps and into the passageway. They disappear and the shouting stops.

The tomb must be filled and sealed quickly as the weather can change without notice. An unexpected storm can bring raging torrents of water down the rocky hillside and possibly flood the small tomb. Also, continuing civil unrest and this current threat of more violence creates a sense of urgency to seal the tomb before dark.

Soldiers are stationed at strategic locations. A band of professional female mourners are following the procession. They are crying loudly and rubbing dirt on their heads as custom dictates. As they arrive in front of the tomb, the soldiers order them to keep moving. The mourners don't like the barked orders and retaliate with long, hard stares. After an exchange of harsh words from both sides, the women reluctantly give in.

The conflict has held up the long line. Others need to unload their burdens and be on their way.

"Move along!" shout the soldiers.

There is silence. Many of the onlookers' eyes fill with tears as they see a beautiful golden throne being carried along the road. It is richly adorned with glass, faience and stone inlay. Even though it is outstanding in its brilliant workmanship, it is the carved scene on the back that is tugging at many hearts. It shows their Pharaoh Tutankhamun and his Queen, Ankhesenamun, gazing fondly at one another. She is applying oil to his shoulder in a scene of loving care.

Carefully, and with a sense of reverence, the load bearers descend the staircase of the tomb and disappear with the priceless treasure. A hush falls over the crowd creating a tranquil moment in the warm, still air.

During the period of the preparation of the mummy, a scribe made a sketch of the tomb. Now everything is well organized and there is a proper place for each treasure in the four small rooms of the tomb. There is little space for the more than three thousand objects. It is an enormous undertaking.

A canopied carrier, supported by two long wooden poles resting on the shoulders of four slaves, arrives near the entrance of the tomb. Gently it is

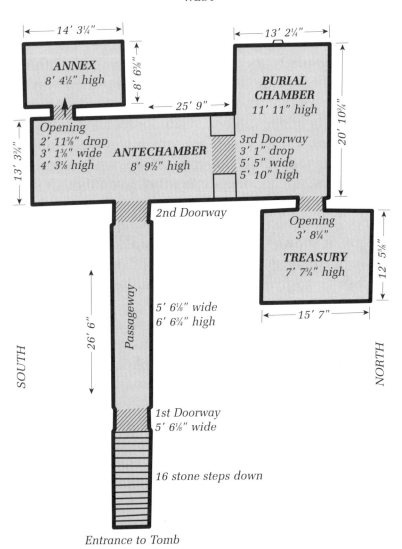

placed on the ground. Ankhesenamun alights. A golden headdress rests securely on top of her head hiding her long black wavy hair underneath. As usual, her eyes are outlined with black kohl creating a doe-like design. Her lids are covered with ground green malachite to help filter the sun's glaring rays. Her petite body is covered with a long filmy white garment that is fastened at her tiny waist. Her petal-soft, olive-colored arms and shoulders are bare. Beautiful pieces of gold jewelry adorn her neck, ears, arms and fingers.

Her dainty sandaled feet glide slowly through the soft sand to the entry. Beneath her, carved from the limestone hill, are the sixteen stone steps. Her delicate hands are clutching a small wreath of fresh olive and willow leaves, blue lotus petals, wild celery and corn-flowers all attached to a circular sheet of papyrus.

Sobbing softly she makes her way carefully down the steps and finds herself going through the short passageway that leads into the first small room of the tomb, the **ANTECHAMBER**.

This room has been designated to hold the king's furniture — beds, chairs, stools, his throne — food, clothing, jewelry, vases, bouquets of flowers, needed transportation, etc., approximately seven hundred objects.

She steps through the doorway of this first room. Facing her is a pile of white oval boxes. They contain the food Tut will need — mummified ducks and other fowl.

Through teary eyes she sees the three great gilded couches — one of which was used at the "House of Vigor" to prepare the mummy. They are strange in appearance. Their four sides are carved in the form of monstrous animals — the first is lion-headed, the second cow-headed and the third is half hippopotamus and half-crocodile. In Egyptian style, there is no "headboard," only a "footboard." Since the couches are tall, there is ample space underneath for the array of chests, stools, staves, vases, etc.

Anie looks at the beautiful chests. They are made of ebony, ivory and wood, inlaid with turquoise, lapis lazuli, carnelian, quartz and serpentine. She recalls when she had supervised what would be placed in them. Some hold her beloved's clothing including special throne robes, one of which is a leopard skin with gold and silver stars and a gold leopard head inlaid with colored glass. Another robe has three thousand gold rosettes attached to it. There are three pairs of court sandals elaborately worked in gold. She insisted that a gold head rest be included as well as a scarab of gold and lapis lazuli blue glass, a buckle of sheet gold with decoration of a hunting scene, a scepter in solid gold and lapis lazuli glass, some beautiful collarettes and necklaces of faience, a handful of massive gold rings wrapped in a piece of linen, some fans and a pair of gloves.

Other chests hold shirts and undergarments, sticks, bows and arrows and a corset with several thousand pieces of gold, glass and faience.

To identify what is in each chest, the contents are listed in hieroglyphs on top.

Casting her eyes upward, she sees the golden throne stacked precariously on top of one of the couches. She remembers when they had posed for the scene that is carved on the back. This is a difficult moment for her.

Needed transportation for the king rests in the corner to her left. Four of the six chariots used by Tut — some for hunting and some for war – are included. Two other chariots have been placed in the treasury. Since they were too large to get through the doorways of the tomb, they had to be dismantled — the axles sawed in half. There are wonderful hunting scenes painted in gold on one. Tut loved to fish and hunt.

Also to the left, under one of the couches, is a small opening. This leads into the second room of the tomb, the **ANNEX**.

Since the opening is not very large, small statured workers entered the room and others passed the 300 or so objects to them.

This room is designated to store the oils, foods and wines, but many other objects are jammed into it since all four rooms of the tomb are so small.

Anie is informed that this room is filled. It holds forty pottery wine jars, thirty-five heavy alabaster vessels containing the precious oils and unguents, one hundred and sixteen baskets of fruit.

There is furniture — stools, chairs, bedsteads — one a folding bedstead — footstools, and hassocks. Also boxes, chests, four headrests and gaming boards.

Some of the boxes contain figures, toys, shields, bows and arrows and other missiles, representing only a part of the many treasures in this room.

There is a special object that Anie cherished. It is a small boat of alabaster, carved with figures of a lion and of a bleating ibex. It had been a gift from Tut to her on their first anniversary.

Knowing that time is passing quickly she makes her way to the next room to her right, the **BURIAL CHAMBER,** where the entombment ceremony is taking place.

Before she steps down into this special room, there, on each side of the large opening, facing each other, are two life-sized, gold-covered wooden statues in the likeness of Tut, but with their skin painted black. Black denotes rebirth. Short, gilded skirts are molded to their bodies and they both hold staffs and maces of gold. Their eyes, set with obsidian, reflect soft rays of light from slow burning oil lamps placed around the room. Their gold-sandaled feet stand rigid on the hard stone floor as if to show their sentinel authority.

Walking slowly between the statues she descends three feet on a temporary set of steps into the holy room. This is also a small room but its ceiling is almost twelve feet high.

The painters have completed their work of religious text on the walls in bright colors. The dead king Tutankhamun is depicted as the God Osiris, King of the Underworld and Lord of the Dead. High Priest Ay is performing the ritual of the "Opening of the Mouth" to the standing mummy so that it might regain its power of speech and also be able to partake of food and drink offerings that will be presented to it.

Turning to the east wall she sees another scene. It shows the king's mummy on its sledge being dragged to the tomb by couriers and high officials.

Small recesses have been chiseled out of the walls and the priests are placing small objects of religious significance in them, conforming with the ritual laid down in the "Book of the Dead." This is for the defense of the tomb and its owner. As the priests finish, the workers are hiding them from view by plastering over the openings. All the while a priest is chanting and reciting religious verses.

Trying to avert her eyes from the coffin that is present in the middle of the room and moving about as in an invisible vacuum, oblivious to those around her, Anie makes her way to a small opening to her right. Bending down slightly, she finds herself peering into a brief entryway, which opens abruptly into another room, the **TREASURY**.

As in other rooms of the tomb, its walls and ceiling are not smooth. It is now completely filled with many gorgeous black shrine-like chests with a number of model boats placed carefully on top. Caskets and vaulted boxes stand silently in their specially assigned places, positioned proudly, and all containing treasures beyond belief.

Holding the small wreath of flowers to her breast, Anie settles her gaze on a massive gilded wooden shrine that has been placed in the center of the room. It is surmounted by a cornice of sacred cobras. She knows that inside is the magnificent alabaster canopic chest resting on a gilded wooden sledge. Hewn in the interior of the chest are four cavities, holding the mummified internal organs of the king. Each organ has been placed in a miniature solid gold coffin inlaid with colored glass and carnelian, wrapped in linen and made to look similar to the second coffin in the holy room. An alabaster stopper, carved in the likeness of the king, has been placed on top of each cavity. A linen pall has been placed over this.

Anie notices four free-standing gold statues. These represent the goddesses of the dead. How very lovely and gracious-looking they are with their arms outstretched toward a shrine as if to protect the sacred contents. At first they seem to appear nude, but a second glance reveals that they are wearing long transparent robes painted over their well-developed young bodies.

Anie glances again to the right side of the room. She knows the contents of the large number of black shrine-like chests. There is one with folding doors, sealed now, that contains statuettes of Tut standing on the backs of black leopards. They have been wrapped carefully in linen.

In front of one of the chests is a wooden model of a granary filled with grain. This is to insure that bread can be made in the afterlife.

To the left is a row of treasure chests beautifully ornamented with ivory, ebony and gesso-gilt. Some of the vaulted boxes are of plain wood painted white. They contain jewelry. One has an ostrich-feathered fan with an ivory handle.

Also on the left side are a number of other objects, including a richly ornamented bow-case, two hunting chariots — their dismembered parts stacked one upon another in a similar manner to those in the first room.

There are ten black wooden kiosks housing the Shawabti figures. These Shawabties are the "answerers" and will answer roll call for the deceased in the hereafter, and also do whatever work is asked of them.

In this room, the shrine equipment is to safeguard the deceased's passage through the Underworld. The objects required for use in his daily life will hence continue in his future life — jewelry for his adornment and chariots for his recreation. The figures of gods are to help him through the dangers to which he may be exposed, and boats to enable him to follow Ra, the Sun-god, on his nocturnal voyage through the interconnecting tunnels of the Underworld and his triumphal journey across the heavens.

Boats symbolize the funeral pilgrimage. A saddle-stone is supplied for grinding corn, and strainers for the preparation of beer. Natron is for the preservation of mortal and immortal remains. All of this, and more, is placed in the tomb.

But Anie also knows what her heart tells to be most important of all. Her two "treasures" of life are each preserved in tiny coffins. One is her first born, and the other is her second born — the two daughters that she and Tut created. How sad, she reflects, that neither premature baby had survived. The first one she had carried only five months; the second, about seven months.

And now, the last item is placed in the small passageway in front of her. It is the figure of the jackal god Anubis, lying upon his shrine. He is swathed in a linen cloth and rests upon a portable sled. Behind him is the head of a bull upon a stand — both emblems of the Underworld.

Before Anie can dwell any longer she feels a slight tug at her arm and hears a gentle low voice asking her to remove herself from the opening.

She backs away from the room filled with the special treasures and once again finds herself in the holy room.

In the center of the room she sees the magnificent yellow quartzite sarcophagus. Its corners rest upon alabaster slabs. Guardian goddesses have been carved on each of the four corners and so placed that

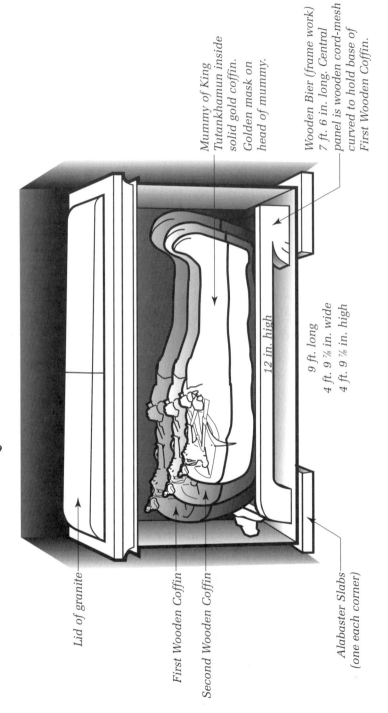

their full spread wings and outstretched arms encircle it with their protective embrace. There are more protective symbols around the base.

On the long voyage to the tomb, the lid of rose granite —tinted to match the sarcophagus — fell from the sledge and was damaged. It is outside the tomb now being mended. The crack across the middle of the lid is being sealed with cement and painted.

Previously, several strong men had lined up on each side of the one and one-fourth ton quartzite sarcophagus and had carefully placed it on a large sledge, with rollers, and had slid it down on wooden planks into the tomb. From the **ANTECHAMBER** it was again placed on another series of wooden planks and slid down into the the **BURIAL CHAMBER**.

Placed first inside this stone sarcophagus — directly on the stone floor of the tomb — is a gold bed-shaped bier. It is a framework made of wood with a lion's head and feet. The heavy wood is covered with gesso-gilt and stands about twelve inches high, is seven feet six inches long and curves to hold and fit the base of the outermost coffin. The central panel is designed to represent a cord-mesh. Besides being an excellent quality of wood, the joinery work is outstanding — it has to be as it is going to have to support the weight of three great coffins weighing more than a ton and a quarter — support them for a long, long time.

Of the three coffins, two made of wood and one made of solid gold, the bottom half of the first wooden coffin had been brought into the tomb and placed on the wooden bier.

Then the bottom half of the second wooden coffin arrives and is placed inside the bottom half of the first wooden coffin.

The solid gold coffin, because of its tremendous weight is handled the same as was the stone sarcophagus. It is placed on a sledge and then slid down planks into the first room of the tomb, rolled to the entrance of the holy room and then lowered down the three steps. Wooden planks are used to support it.

Several strong men had lined up on each side, and with a system of pulleys and ropes, had placed it inside the bottom of the second wooden coffin.

Needless to say, this was a gigantic undertaking.

To make it difficult for tomb robbers to reach the mummy, a priest has driven silver nails into secret places around each coffin as it is fitted into place.

Before the lid of the second coffin is placed over the gold coffin, one of the priests pours about two buckets of black, pleasant-smelling oil over the gold coffin, avoiding only the areas of the face and feet. He recites more religious text.

The mummy of Tutankhamun lies silent in the solid gold coffin. He faces east so he will be able to see the rising sun.

Anie walks slowly to the center of the room. The lid of the second coffin has now been placed over the solid gold coffin and rests on its own bottom half, thus hiding the gold coffin from view.

She stares down at the beautiful wooden coffin. It is heavily gilded and designed to show two winged goddesses — Isis and Neith — enclasping the body. The hands are crossed over the heart, the right holding the emblematic flail, and the left the crooked scepter. Both are made of gold and faience.

Two emblems protrude from the forehead. They are symbols of Upper and Lower Egypt — a vulture and a cobra. The face is carved in the likeness of the young pharaoh Tutankhamun.

Ay painstakingly places a gossamer linen sheet over the face and shoulders of the coffin. Then he reads from the "Book of the Dead," reciting necessary instructions for the deceased.

When Ay is finished, Anie very gently places her wreath of flowers on top of the linen pall. She can see through the sheer covering. The eyes of obsidian stare up at her. Tears flow down her cheeks.

Anie murmurs: "These flowers will be with you forever to remind you of my love. You will know that I will always be your **"Flower of the Nile."**

16

ENTOMBMENT, INTRIGUE AND FLIGHT

Releasing her grasp on the wreath of flowers, Ankhesenamun feels as though a heavy burden has been lifted from her whole being. She realizes that the past is a yesterday. The good times of her past life will always remain with her — in her heart and in her mind.

As a mature woman in her early twenties she knows that there is still much time left in her life for happiness and adventure. A new life is now awaiting her at an unknown destination with Anwar, Tashery, Farida and Tahlia.

She turns to leave. The chanting verses of the priests echo in her ears and the incense hangs like a heavy fog in the dimly lit room.

Grandfather Ay stands close to her side. He is supervising the final stages of the royal burial. The top of the first wooden coffin is now being placed on its bottom half covering the second wooden coffin. It has been carved and decorated to look much like the second with a golden effigy of the young boy king. It reveals magnificent workmanship and the finest sculpture. The face and hands are in sheet gold, the eyes of aragonite and obsidian, the eyebrows and eyelids inlaid with lapis lazuli glass and upon the forehead — as on the other coffins — the two Egyptian emblems of the cobra and vulture delicately worked in brilliant inlay.

The entire coffin had first been covered with a thin layer of plaster and then overlaid with sheet gold. Narrow strips of gold were then soldered to the base to form cells in which small pieces of colored glass, fixed with cement, were laid.

Anie can't keep her eyes off of the beautiful coffin. The colors are so vibrant — red, light and dark shades of blue, lilac tones all set in the small cells. They cover the entire coffin.

Again, a priest places a shroud over the gold face and shoulders and gently lays a wreath of flowers on top.

The mended lid of the quartzite sarcophagus is now being carried into the holy room. Very carefully it is lifted and placed on the stone sarcophagus, hiding from view the precious coffins it is to cover and to protect.

Ay turns to Anie and looks deeply into her eyes. She can't help noticing how he has aged. Not only does the gray hair at his temples reveal advanced years, but she notices new deep lines and wrinkles in his face that she had not observed before. Only his eyes have not changed. Inner peace and contentment shine through them. As the High Priest of Egypt he has done his work well with honor and sincerity. And now, as Pharaoh, Anie knows he will have an honest reign. It won't be a dictatorial reign, since that is not Ay's style. She knows that her grandfather will lead the people well — if given the chance. His work is indeed cut out for him.

"The assembling and erecting of the four floorless shrines is to take place now. Since this is such a small room, I suggest that you wait in the **ANTECHAMBER**."

Anie nods in agreement as Ay assists her up the steps.

The fourth (innermost) shrine is being brought through the doorway of the first room. Anie steps out of the way, goes to the back and stands alongside the disassembled pile of chariots.

This shrine is made in five sections of 2½ inch oak planking. It is lowered into the **BURIAL CHAMBER** and placed over the stone sarcophagus. It rests on the stone floor of the tomb.

Outside the tomb, leaning against the hillside, looking like giant dominoes, are the other sections of oak planking for the third and second shrines (brought into the tomb in that order). One and three-fourth inch heavy cedar panels, are being used for the first (outermost) Great Wooden Shrine, the last to be erected.

Each section has been carefully numbered and oriented to show how it is to be fitted and where. The workers are moving very fast. The crowd is getting more and more restless.

As the rectangular shrines are being assembled, Ay tries to keep order, but much confusion is taking place. In all plans when time is of the essence, mistakes are made. Under pressure, the hurried workers miss their marks and deep dents from their hammers do their damage on some of the wooden planks. But all in all, the carpentry and joinery work of the shrines exhibit great skill. Chips of wood lie on the stone floor.

THE FOUR SHRINES

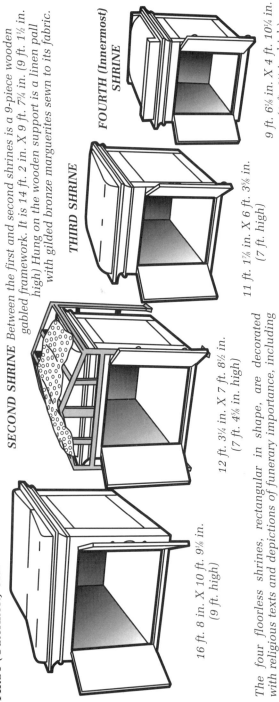

FIRST (Outermost) GREAT WOODEN SHRINE

16 ft. 8 in. X 10 ft. 9⅛ in. (9 ft. high)

SECOND SHRINE Between the first and second shrines is a 9-piece wooden gabled framework. It is 14 ft. 2 in. X 9 ft. 7¾ in. (9 ft. 1½ in. high) Hung on the wooden support is a linen pall with gilded bronze marguerites sewn to its fabric.

12 ft. 3¼ in. X 7 ft. 8½ in. (7 ft. 4⅝ in. high)

THIRD SHRINE

11 ft. 1⅞ in. X 6 ft. 3⅜ in. (7 ft. high)

FOURTH (Innermost) SHRINE

9 ft. 6⅞ in. X 4 ft. 10¼ in. (6 ft. 2⅜ in. high)

The four floorless shrines, rectangular in shape, are decorated with religious texts and depictions of funerary importance, including Book of the Dead instructions.

Most surfaces, both inside and out (and doors), are covered with gold paint and blue faience inlay (on plaster of Paris, called "gesso"). Some walls have beautifully designed grill-work.

The First (outermost) Shrine is constructed of 1⅜ inch heavy cedar panels. The others are made of 2½ inch oak planking. The Second Shrine is in 16 sections, the Third Shrine is in 10 sections and the Fourth Shrine is in 5 sections

The four shrines vary in size from large to small so as to encompass each other in a nesting fashion. The width of the corridors between them varies from about four feet to about eighteen inches. The outermost and second shrine have progressively wider measurements.

Anie sees a familiar object being brought in. It is a perfume vase that Tut had given her, carved of pure semi-translucent alabaster. It is to be placed in front of the door of the third shrine. Also, a beautiful cosmetic jar, made of alabaster, will be placed beside it. The design is that of a recumbent lion with a red tongue. As many other things are being carried in — those which she and Tut had shared — tears fill her eyes.

The remaining sections for the second and first shrines are now in the holy room and almost completed. The oak planking is overlaid with superbly delicate gold-work upon plaster with blue faience inlay in the background. These shrines, both inside and out, are covered with religious texts from the "Book of the Dead," figures of deities and symbols connected with the Underworld.

On top of the second shrine a linen pall is placed with gilt bronze marguerites sewn to its fabric. It is held on a wooden support. The wood is olive (from Egypt) and persea (from Abyssinia). Both woods are considered sacred, symbolizing Tut's power at home and over foreign lands.

The OUTERMOST GREAT WOODEN SHRINE is assembled and looks like a golden tabernacle. It is similar in design and even more brilliant in workmanship than the others. There are more hieroglyphs surrounded by a series of hawks with wings

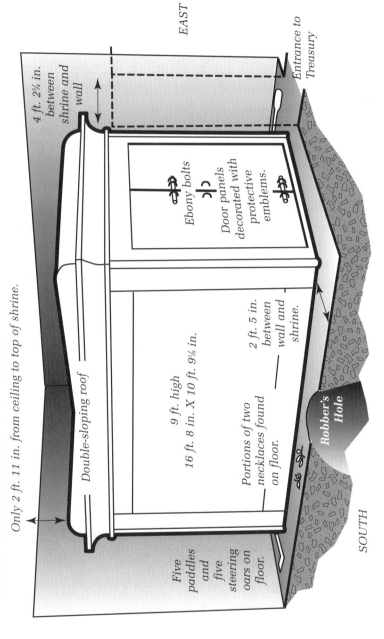

outspread that appear to lovingly protect the body of the king.

As Anie sees the completion of the Great Wooden Shrine, she walks to the opening of the Holy Room and reads from a portion of the text: *"I have seen yesterday; I know tomorrow."*

Returning to her place in the **ANTECHAMBER**, she dwells on what she has just read. In her heart she knows Tut will be loved in his afterlife.

Before each set of folding doors is closed and sealed, many more objects are placed in the narrow corridors on either side and between the shrines. There are numerous ceremonial maces, sticks, staves and bows — some carefully wrapped in linen. There is a series of curved batons and gold and silver sticks with tiny statuettes of the youthful monarch. A "reed" is included. The hieroglyphs indicate, *"which His Majesty cut with his own hand."*

Remainder of the treasures are of a more ceremonial and religious kind such as scepters and crooked and forked sticks made of wood covered with gesso and gilt.

Two remarkable ostrich-feather fans are placed between the second and outermost shrines. One is made of ebony overlaid with gold and encrusted with semiprecious stones; the other is of wood inlaid with gold. The palm of one has a hunting scene of the king on the front, and on the back is a scene of Tut in his chariot.

The second and third shrine doors are bolted and sealed, and the great folding doors of the outermost great shrine are closed and bolted. but not sealed. Winged figures of tutelary goddesses of the dead painted on the doors are to help protect the dead pharaoh.

COMPLETION OF BURIAL

- First (outermost) Great Wooden Shrine
- Linen Pall
- Fourth (innermost) Shrine
- Quartzite Sarcophagus
- Wooden Bier
- Solid Gold Coffin and Mummy of Tutankhamun
- Second Wooden Coffin
- First Wooden Coffin
- Wooden Framework
- Second Shrine
- Alabaster Slabs (one each corner)
- Third Shrine

The **OUTERMOST GREAT WOODEN SHRINE** is so large it almost fills the chamber. The cornice top reaches to within 2 feet 11 inches of the ceiling.

Ay is instructing the workers to place the last items around the four sides of the Great Shrine.

In front of the massive folding doors of the Great Shrine, and just after the ebony bolts are joined together, an exquisite triple-lamp of floral form, carved out of a single block of translucent alabaster in the shape of three lotiform cups, is placed. A number of funerary emblems are placed around the shrine, in the corners and on the ground. Some are strange in appearance.

At the western end in the northern and southern corners are golden emblems of Anubis. He hangs on lotiform poles about six feet in height, set in alabaster pots and placed on reed mats.

A holy man chants: *"These emblems are to guide our beloved Pharaoh through this domain — for was not Anubis, the Jackal, a prowler of the dead and did not Ra send him forth to bury Osiris?"*

There are objects carved of wood — one a sacred goose varnished black and wrapped in linen. It is placed along the east wall beside two rush-work baskets.

At the southwest corner an immense funerary bouquet of twigs and branches of the persea and olive is placed.

A priest leans down and arranges five paddles and five steering oars on the floor between the Great Shrine and the north wall. These the king will need to ferry himself across the waters of the Underworld.

Ay stares at one of the two alabaster vases that have just been placed on the floor — the last objects to be in this holy room. Beside the vase is a religious emblem bound in papyrus and a lotus flower. The two symbolize the union of the "Two Lands" or "Kingdoms" of Upper and Lower Egypt. Its hieroglyphs indicate, "Myriad of Years."

Some of these articles express fine art in the service of religious beliefs. Mingled with a fear of the very gods and demons of their own creation, the Egyptians are sincere in their feelings and affection for the dead. Ay is very aware of this as his own feelings are so strong in his love for his grandson, Tut, that it is difficult for him to bear.

The workers file out of the tomb. The priests stand in a last reverent bow. Lamps are now ready to be extinguished. Without anyone noticing, Ay silently leaves the holy room and enters the **ANTECHAMBER**.

In a dim corner Anie is still waiting as she had been instructed. Ay walks to her side.

As she begins to talk to him she feels a gentle touch to her arm from behind. Turning, she is taken by surprise to see a familiar black, kind face smiling at her.

Anie is so startled that it takes her a moment to regain her composure.

"Tahlia, what are you doing here?" Before Tahlia can answer, Anie adds: "You are supposed to be on the yacht!"

Dark, anxious eyes stare back at her. There is no reply.

Anie's eyes glance downward at the figure standing close to her. She swallows hard. Tahlia is wearing the same clothing as she, except for a large linen shawl covering her head and shoulders.

"And why are you dressed like me?" Anie asks anxiously.

"My dear, listen carefully." Tahlia is trying to settle Anie down.

"We don't have much time!" "The crowd outside is getting more hostile and your safety is in jeopardy."

Handing Anie the large shawl as she removes the gold head piece, Tahlia continues:

"Use this to cover your head, face and shoulders as you leave."

Tahlia adds in a stern voice: "Don't speak to anyone!" "There is a carriage at the entrance of the tomb."

Anie takes the shawl from her. She starts to speak.

"No — listen —- !" urges Tahlia.

"It was not Ay who murdered Akhenaton." There is a brief pause.

"It was I who placed the cobra in his room."

"But Tahlia, everyone believed that Ay had arranged the incident." Anie is astounded at the statement.

"It is difficult for me to believe this!"

"I am the guilty one," confesses Tahlia."

"The people know the truth now, but they think because I was your servant you had ordered me to do it. Akenaton's die-hard followers are determined to destroy you as you leave the tomb."

"That is why you must leave at once!"

A bewildered Anie turns to Ay. He nods in agreement.

"Everything she is telling you is the truth."

Tahlia grabs Anie and holds her in her strong arms — knowing that this is the last time she will feel that warm embrace. Anie does not want to be released.

Words between them are not necessary.

Ay pulls a still puzzled and crying Anie away from Tahlia. He places the shawl over her head and shoulders.

"Remember to keep your face covered — only your eyes can be visible."

Assisted by Ay, Anie stumbles through the room to the exit.

Ay gazes deeply down into the wide, anxious eyes. He kisses Anie softly on the cheek and whispers: "Good-bye, my sweet one."

He adds: "Take care of Tashery and Anwar — they need you."

Tears welling in his eyes, he waves a farewell: "May a new world bring to you the happiness you so deserve."

As Anie runs quickly through the narrow passageway she finds herself at the bottom of the sixteen stone steps that lead up and out of the tomb.

Lifting the long dress and covering herself with the shawl as directed she begins the climb upward.

The crowd outside is so busy bickering and arguing with one another that they pay no attention to the figure leaving the tomb. Anie goes unnoticed.

The awaiting carriage whisks her away down the dusty road that leads to the river.

From the rolling carriage she can hear the crowd behind in the distance. Their voices are becoming louder and more intense in anger. Glancing backward, Anie sees them moving toward the entrance to the tomb.

A woman's scream is heard. It is filled with pain as it pierces the very depths of the Valley of the Kings.

Like the settling of dust, the voices become hushed. Then there is silence.

"Tahlia!" screams Anie.

Her body aches in desperation. She knows the gods have played their parts — only too well. There is nothing she can do.

A small sailing vessel is waiting at the riverbank and Anie is rushed to it. Swiftly they cross the Nile to Thebes.

And there, at the shore, awaiting in all its splendor, is the royal yacht. It has been stripped of its insignia. The passengers and crew are waiving and yelling — anxious to be on their way.

As Anie ascends the gangplank, she looks up. Two lone figures are standing on the deck, looking down at her. One is a small child and the other a tall, dark handsome man.

"Tashery!" "Anwar!"

Remorse leaves her almost as suddenly as it had overtaken her. Looking at them, she is filled with overwhelming love and joy. "There is always hope," she murmurs to herself.

Halfway up the gangplank Anie glances down at the water. A single lotus flower appears. It is in full bloom. She gazes at it for a moment and thinks about her beloved Tut and how he held her as his "FLOWER OF THE NILE."

Now she realizes the significance of life compared to a flower — the beginning, the growing, the joys, the sorrows — and most important of all — the seeds left behind.

She sighs, "We are all like a 'FLOWER OF THE NILE.'"

A FLOWER

The seed of a flower is planted in the earth to be reborn,
Then struggles upward out of the darkness for a place to adorn.
As it grows very slowly, a bud forms in the center,
And hopes that into a world of fascination it shall enter.

Nourished by nature with sun and rain in all its glory,
It wants to begin a new life as written in a good story.
But when life begins and continues until full bloom,
The flower realizes that it is in store for some gloom.

It's those happy and contented days in the sun,
That help to erase the bad and make room for fun,
Attaining full bloom, its beauty is something to behold,
Existence on earth is now complete with many tales untold.

In the end, plucked for greatness is for some,
However, most only inherit Paradise to come.
But the seeds which are left behind still smile,
For they know the secret of life is worthwhile.

Doris Auger Davis

APPENDIX

HISTORIC EVENTS DURING ANCIENT EGYPTIAN TIMES

B.C.

2700 B.C.:	City of Heliopolis (ancient On) 7 miles north of Cairo site of world's oldest university. Later students included Moses, Herodotus and Plato. Founded this date.
2700-2300 B.C.:	Pyramids of Egypt
1900 B.C.:	Egyptians make first convenient writing material from papyrus.
1600 B.C.:	Hittites conquer Babylon. Egyptians begin using horses.
1500-1400 B.C.:	Moses (Ten Commandments given); Joshua; Exodus from Egypt. Thutmose III rules Egypt – wheel used first time in Egypt. Shang Dynasty flourishes in China (1766-1123 B.C.).
1333-1323 B.C.:	**Tutankhamun, King of Egypt**
1200-1100 B.C.:	Deborah, Gideon, Ruth, Eli. Trojan War Ramses III, Ruler of Egypt – end of great Egyptian empire
1000 B.C.:	Saul, David, Solomon
900-700 B.C.:	Two Kingdoms – Israel (North); Juda (South) Olympic Games begin in Greece (776 B.C.) Rome founded
600-400 B.C.:	Nebuchadnezzar II reigns (605-562 B.C.)and builds the Hanging Gardens in Babylon Confucius lives in China (551-479 B.C.) Persian Rule begins Socrates lives in Greece (470-399 B.C.) Buddha lives in India (Gautama Buddha 563-483 B.C.) End of Old Testament
480 B.C.	Great Wall of China - building begins (21 centuries and 1,500 miles to complete)

375-175 B.C.:	Greek Rule – Plato, Aristotle Parthenon in Athens Alexander the Great (356-323 B.C.) reaches Alexandria; 332 B.C.
69-30 B.C.:	Cleopatra VII, Queen of Egypt, loved by Julius Caesar and Mark Antony
50 B.C.:	Roman Rule Herod becomes King of the Jews

A.D.

1-4 A.D.:	Mary and Joseph flee to Egypt with baby Jesus
5 A.D.:	Jesus lives in Nazareth with Mary and Joseph
25 A.D.:	John the Baptist begins to preach Jesus is baptized and begins ministry
30 A.D.:	Peter (Church established on Pentecost - Acts 2)
33 A.D.:	Death, burial and resurrection of Jesus
69 A.D.:	Caesar Augustus becomes first emperor of Rome Egyptians embrace Christianity in Alexandria after the preaching of St. Mark the Evangelist. "Copts"
79 A.D.:	Mount Vesuvius erupts and buries Pompeii
65 A.D.:	Peter executed by Nero. Paul executed at Rome.
95 A.D.:	John – Revelation written on Isle of Patmos
100 A.D.:	Death of Apostle John. City of Rome burned during reign of Nero; Persecution of Christians begins. (37-68 A.D.) Colosseum is built. (72-80 A.D.)
300 A.D.:	Yucatan Peninsula near Cuba (Cancun, Cozumel) erect massive monuments; use stone tools and without wheel.
900 A.D.:	Mayan civilization in Mexico peaks (then declines abruptly).

ANCIENT EGYPTIAN TRADITIONAL CHRONOLOGY

The dates and Dynasties vary, depending upon the research of numerous scholars.

The chronology shown on this page is considered to be traditional and is used in most publications.

The chronology used in this story does not always follow the traditional approach.

The Author

	DYNASTY	YEAR
PREHISTORIC AGE	"0"	4500 B.C.
ARCHAIC PERIOD	1st, 2nd, 3rd	3100–2613 B.C.
OLD KINGDOM	4th, 5th, 6th	2613–2181 B.C.
FIRST INTERMEDIATE PERIOD	7th, 8th, 9th, 10th	2181–2040 B.C.
MIDDLE KINGDOM	11th, 12th	2133–1786 B.C.
END OF MIDDLE KINGDOM	13th, 14th	1786–1603 B.C.
SECOND INTERMEDIATE PERIOD	15th, 16th, 17th	1720–1567 B.C.
NEW EMPIRE	**18th, 19th, 20th**	**1567–1085 B.C.**
	(Tutankhamun 1371–1353 B.C.)	
	(Ramses II 1304–1237 B.C.)	
END OF THE NEW EMPIRE	21st, 22nd, 23rd 24th, 25th, 26th	1085–525 B.C.
PERSIAN DOMINATION	27th, 28th, 29th, 30th	525–343 B.C.
SECOND PERSIAN DOMINATION	31st	343–335 B.C.

Alexander The Great reaches Alexandria – 332 B.C.
Ptolemy I crowned Pharaoh – 304 B.C.

THE DISCOVERY

EGYPT — NOVEMBER 4, 1922 — At the entrance of the Valley of the Kings, five and one-half miles from the Nile River, an Englishman by the name of Howard Carter and his crew of Egyptian workers removed tons of sand, dirt and debris and uncovered an ancient burial place. It was the tomb of King Tutankhamun.

Fifteen years earlier, an American archeologist named Theodore Davis had been excavating near this same site and had found a light blue varnished pitcher with the name of Tutankhamun on it. The hieroglyphs on the royal cartouche spelled out "Nebkheperura," his throne name. Then the following year, in 1907, about seven yards below ground, some of the items he and his colleagues found included a broken wooden box containing several leaves of embossed gold upon which were the silhouettes and names of "Touatankhamanon and Ankhousanamanon." There were pieces of pottery — one a long-necked wine bottle. The stoppered lids on some pots had the name of the young pharaoh on the seal. One was wrapped in a piece of cloth dated "Year 6" of his reign. Also, there was a heap of linen used for embalming and wrapping the mummy, and three semicircular handkerchiefs (or wig covers). With all of this evidence found, could this possibly be the remains of King Tutankhamun's tomb? The question was accepted as a realistic one for many years. Besides, no other tombs discovered in the area had ever revealed significant artifacts. The tomb robbers had done their job diligently over the centuries by ransacking and carrying away the great treasures.

But it was Howard Carter, born in 1873 at Norfolk, England, who had never given up hope of finding the actual tomb, believing it was still buried somewhere in the Valley of the Kings. No antiquities from that tomb had ever come on the market. Even so, some of his colleagues thought him foolish to pursue this belief of an undiscovered tomb.

Carter knew that tombs of all the other rulers of the 18th and 19th Dynasties in the Valley of the Kings had been accounted for, and firmly believed that Tutankhamun's still remained undiscovered.

It was not a haphazard digging. Carter and his crew of Egyptians had toiled for six full seasons, eliminating one possibility after another of its location. Also, without the financial and moral support of Lord Carnarvon, a wealthy Englishman and friend, the year after year of digging would not have been possible. In the sixth year, even Lord Carnarvon was beginning to lose faith in Carter. To try to finance the sixth year himself would have been very difficult for Carter, but he told Lord Carnarvon he would try. Carnarvon decided to continue his financial backing for one more season.

The rest is history.

HOWARD CARTER

Egyptological discoveries were not new to Howard Carter. From 1907 to 1911 he discovered many important tombs in Egypt. In 1914 he unearthed the long-sought tomb of King Amenhotep I of the 18th Dynasty, cleared the interior of the tomb of Amenophis III in 1915, and in 1916 discovered the extraordinary Cliff Tomb of Queen Hatshepsut.

He also excelled in drawing and painting. In fact, he went to Egypt first as an archeological illustrator. He exercised his artistic talents in the drawing of scenes and inscriptions for epigraphic purposes in the production of painted facsimiles of colored reliefs and scenes, in topographical and imaginative water colors, and in the reproduction of objects found in the course of excavation. From 1893 to 1900 he had three volumes of his work published in the form of colored facsimiles. Some of his best water-color paintings, mostly of zoological details, were from the tomb of Khnumhotpe.

He traced scenes and inscriptions from Middle Kingdom tombs of Beni Hasan and El-Bersha.

Carter had no formal education. He received little in the way of formal honors. He was never honored by the British monarch. Recognition was made for his professional achievement by a Yale doctorate, and he was presented a Corresponding Membership in the Royal Academy of History, Madrid, Spain.

On March 2, 1939 in London, he died at the age of sixty-six. The causes of death were cardiac failure and lymphadenoma (Hodgkin's disease). The debilitating condition of his health caused him to lead a painful and miserable existence for ten years before he died. A niece, Phyllis Walker, helped to care for him.

He never married.

His life was devoted to Egypt and archaeology.

He spent ten years clearing the tomb of Tutankhamun.

One thing for certain, we can all be thankful that it was such a man as Howard Carter who discovered the tomb of Tutankhamun. After the opening, he continually insisted upon the most exacting and meticulous treatment of each and every treasure — much to the dismay of local authorities. Visitors from around the world and the news media interrupted the important work many times.

But his efforts have made it possible for many people from all the continents to view, study and appreciate these wonderful works of art that reveal to us many things about an ancient people and civilization.

In spite of his unusual life, what a fantastic experience it must have been when he, Lord Carnarvon and his daughter Evelyn, all stood in front of the sealed tomb door... entrance into another time.

After a hole was made in the door and a candle inserted, Lord Carnarvon asked: "Can you see anything?"

Carter replied: "Yes — wonderful things!"

BIBLIOGRAPHY

THE DISCOVERY OF THE TOMB OF TUTANKHAMEN
by Howard Carter and A. C. Mace
Originally published 1923 (Volume I);
republished 1977

THE TOMB OF TUTANKHAMEN
by Howard Carter
Original edition 1927 Volume II; Volume III 1933
Copyright 1954 (First published in U.S.A. 1992)
(Also Volume II, 1963, Cooper Square Publishers, Inc., New York)

THE MUMMY
by E. A. Wallis Budge
Copyright 1974 by Causeway Books; a facsimile of the second edition 1894

EGYPT, GIFT OF THE NILE
by Walter A. Fairservic, Jr.
Copyright 1963

HOWARD CARTER, The Path to Tutankhamun
by T. G. H. James
Copyright 1992 by Kegan Paul International Ltd, England

TUTANKHAMUN, His Tomb and its Treasures
by I. E. S. Edwards
Copyright 1976 (beautiful pictures in color)

ENCYCLOPEDIA BRITANNICA

TUTANKHAMEN (Life and Death of a Pharaoh)
by Christiane Desroches-Noblecourt
Copyright 1963

TUTANKHAMUN, THE UNTOLD STORY
by Thomas Hoving
Copyright 1978 by Hoving Associates, Inc.
Published by Simon & Schuster, New York
Photographs by Metropolitan Museum of Art, Copyright 1979

THE PYRAMIDS
by Ahmed Fakhry
Copyright 1961 by the University of Chicago
First published 1961; Second Edition 1969

THE LOST PHARAOHS
by Leonard Cottrell
Copyright 1961

ANCIENT EGYPT
by Lionel Casson, Professor of Classics,
New York University Copyright 1965 Time, Inc.
(Time-Life Books, New York)

THE CULTURE OF ANCIENT EGYPT
by John A. Wilson
Copyright 1951 by The University of Chicago

**MUMMIES, MYTH AND MAGIC
IN ANCIENT EGYPT**
by Christine El Mahdy
Copyright 1989, Text and Layout, Thames and
Hudson, Ltd, London
First published in U.S.A. 1989 by Thames and
Hudson, Inc., New York

ANCIENT EGYPT: A SOCIAL HISTORY
by B. G. Trigger, B. J. Kemp, D. O'Connor and
A. B. Lloyd
Copyright 1983, Cambridge University Press
Reprinted 1984, 1985, 1986, 1987, 1989 and 1990

THE SEARCH FOR THE GOLD OF TUTANKHAMEN
by Arnold C. Brackman
Copyright 1976, Mason/Charter, New York

EGYPTIAN MUMMIES
by Carol Andres
Copyright 1984, Trustees of the British Museum
by British Museum Publications

**The Complete TUTANKHAMUN,
The King – The Tomb – The Royal Treasure**
by Nicholas Reeves
Copyright 1990 Thames and Hudson Ltd, London
Text Copyright 1990 Nicholas Reeves
First published in U.S.A. 1990 by Thames and
Hudson Inc., New York
Reprinted 1993

THE GODS OF THE EGYPTIANS
by E. A. Wallis Budge
This Dover Edition, first published in 1969,
is an unabridged republication of the work
originally published by The Open Court
Publishing Company, Chicago, and Methuen &
Company, London, in 1904 (Volume 2)
Library of Congress Catalog Card Number
72-91925

GLOSSARY

Amun: Patron god of Thebes. The principal god of Egypt during the New Kingdom period. It's symbol was often that of a ram.

Ankh: A symbol to represent eternal life, in the form of a loop and a handle.

Anubis: The god of embalming — the jackal-headed son of Osiris.

Aswan High Dam: Built in 1964 A.D. to harness the Nile River.

Aton: A universal power whose symbol was the sun. The controversial Aton cult achieved its popularity during the reign of Pharaoh Akenaton.

Bier: A wooden frame work. (The central panel is wooden cord-mesh that is curved to hold the base of the First Wooden Coffin).

"Brood" Gold: This use of the term "brood gold" by Howard Carter probably comes from the Old English "bhreu," meaning to cut or to break-up.

Calendar: Egyptian Calendar introduced about 4241 B.C. They overlooked or ignored the fact that every four years Sirus rose a day later. The star year, which is virtually identical with the solar year, measures about 365¼ days.

Carnelian: A pale to deep red or reddish-brown variety of clear chalcedony. From cornelle or cornel (cherry). (Chalcedony is a translucent to transparent milky or grayish quartz with distinctive microscopic crystals arranged in slender fibers in parallel bands). A mystical stone.

Cloisonné: Egyptian cloisonné is not true cloisonné in that the glass is already shaped before being put into the cells. In true cloisonné, the cells are filled with enamel paste and fused in place.

Electrum: An alloy of gold and silver.

Faience: Glazed and decorated pottery. Made with a paste of powdered quartz (rather than clay) and was coated with a vitreous (glassy) paste. When fired, it took on a beautiful glasslike shine. Earliest examples are all blue; later learned to create green, white, black, violet, red, yellow and even multicolored effects. Made tiny beads, small statues, vases, tiles and figurines.

Ferrule: A metal ring or cap, as on the end of a cane or around the handle of a tool.

Gesso: A ground of plaster, as gypsum or plaster of Paris, prepared to be painted on.

Gild: To cover with gold or gold leaf.

Hathor: A goddess of the Nile and of fertility depicted as having a cow's head.

Hieroglyphics: Development about 3100 B.C. A written language of pictures and symbols by the ancient Egyptians. If the person or animal in the hieroglyph faced to the right, the symbols were read from right to left. Likewise, if the symbol faced left, the hieroglyph was read from left to right. In some instances, the figure faced up or down, indicating the direction in which to read.

Horus: The son of Isis and Osiris. He destroyed Set, the slayer of Osiris. He was also later believed to be the son of Ra and was depicted as a hawk. The eye of Horus, which he lost in the fight with Set, was regarded as having magical properties.

Isis: Wife of Osiris. She was worshiped as the goddess of fertility and motherhood. (Most popular deity of Egypt in Ptolemaic and Roman times).

Karnak: Today, most of the colors are gone, but remnants of the clerestory windows are still visible and the gigantic columns still stand. Only one of Queen Hatshepsut's obelisks remains, minus the beauty of the gilded top. The roof is gone from the great temple. The hieroglyphs have been deciphered revealing three hundred and fifty-nine names of conquered peoples and cities, names from the southern Sudan to north of the Euphrates. Other kings— Ramesses I — and Ramesses II with his memorable Battle of Kadesh, added halls and pylons and obelisks in commemoration of their victories and as thank offerings to their god. In 1949, nine-foot sphinxes were uncovered, linked with the more famous Avenue of Sphinxes which led from the temple of Karnak to the Luxor Temple two miles away.

Kohl: A powder to darken the edges of the eyes. (Usually for cosmetic purposes).

Lapis Luzuli: An opaque, azure-blue to deep-blue gemstone of lazurite. (Lazurite is a relatively rare blue, violet-blue or greenish-blue mineral. Also called lapis lazuli).

Malachite: A mineral of copper carbonate, green or blue-green in color. Used by the Egyptians as <u>eye paint</u>.

Marguerites: "Rosettes." An ornament or badge resembling a rose; a painted or sculptural ornament with parts circularly arranged. A flowerless cluster of leaves, organs, parts arranged in circles. (Somewhat like modern "sequins," but more elaborately designed).

Mastaba: From Arabic "mastabah" meaning "bench."

Myriad: A vast, indefinite number.

Narmer: First identified pharaoh of Egypt. (Probably the "Menes" celebrated by the Greeks as first pharaoh and uniter of Egypt).

Natron: A natural compound of sodium carbonate and bicarbonate with admixtures of sodium sulphate and chloride.

Nefertiti: When Akhtenaton was married to Nefertiti, she bore him six daughters. He later married one of their daughters, Ankhesenamun (Ankhsenpaaton). There is no further mention of Nefertiti in hieroglyphic studies; however, her legacy lives on in her portrait busts, the best known of which is housed in the Dahlem Museum, Berlin.

Nubia: South of Aswan in a narrow valley of the Nile, as far as the second cataract region in the Sudan.

Nut: The sky goddess, depicted as a beautiful woman bending over the earth.

Obsidian: A black, hard, volcanic glass. (Can be made at least 100 times sharper than most surgical steel scalpels presently in use).

Osiris: King of the Underworld and Lord of the Dead. His wife was Isis. Sons were Horus and Anubis. Usually appears in mummy form.

Pall: A cover for a coffin, bier or tomb, often made of black, purple or white velvet. (The material of choice for the ancient Egyptians was linen).

Pectoral: An ornament worn on the breast.

Pharaoh: The name of Egyptian kings and synonymous with kingship. It derives from the Egyptian term Per-aa or "Great House," meaning the palace of the king.

Pyramid, Great: Using the water level for the base of the pyramid, the site is so even that the southeast corner of the pyramid stands only one-half inch higher than the northeast corner today. It is 750 feet square at its base, and 481 feet tall. Today, in the Twentieth Century A.D., the area of its base would hold the total of St. Paul's Cathedral and Westminster Abbey in London, St. Peter's Basilica in Rome, the Florence Cathedral and the Milan Cathedral in Italy. In other words, it would cover the same area as four large modern city blocks. Also, today, its dimensions have been reduced to 746 feet square by 450 feet and, like the Sphinx, the wind and sand continue to beat upon it unmercifully, and the acid from the exhausts of cars, buses and industrial pollution is slowly destroying the limestone covering.

Quartzite: A metamorphic rock resulting from the recrystallization of quartz sandstone.

Ra: The sun god. Probably the most important deity in ancient Egypt. His symbol was the sun's disk, but he had various other forms, such as that of the khepher or scarab beetle. Also known as Re.

Sarcophagus: A stone coffin.

Scarab: A beetle.

Sekhemet: A warlike goddess, usually depicted with the head of a lioness.

Shawabti: (or Ushabti). The "answerers," who will do whatever is asked of them by the deceased in the hereafter. Small models of servants, usually carved in wood, which were placed in the tombs. They were endowed with magical properties.

Sphinx: A man or woman-faced deity with the body of a lion or lioness. The sphinx at Giza was built about 2650 B.C. Its head is thirty feet long and the face fourteen feet wide. The Muhammadan rulers in later years tried to destroy its features — a canon ball hit its mark and blew its nose off.

Tell El Amarna: The author chose this site for the primary residence of the royal family to avoid confusion. The actual palace was "Akhetaton" that Akhenaton had built at Tell El Amarna.

Thebes: Modern Luxor.

Thoth: In Egyptian religion, the god of writing, knowledge and wisdom. Depicted as having an ibis (a long-billed wading bird) head on a human body.

Tutankhamun: It is generally accepted that his age at death was eighteen as autopsies later revealed evidence of the extent of bone union — epiphysis — between the femur and upper end of the Tibia in both thighs and legs. In the arms, the lower ends of the radius and ulna showed little or no union. These findings are common at the age of eighteen.

Tutelary: The function or capacity of a guardian.

Wheel: First used in Egypt about 1500 B.C.